Fannie Isabel Sherrick

**Love or Fame**

And other Poems

Fannie Isabel Sherrick

**Love or Fame**
*And other Poems*

ISBN/EAN: 9783337341916

Printed in Europe, USA, Canada, Australia, Japan

Cover: Foto ©Andreas Hilbeck / pixelio.de

More available books at **www.hansebooks.com**

# LOVE OR FAME;

## AND

## OTHER POEMS.

BY

## FANNIE ISABELLE SHERRICK.

"Fame is the thirst of youth."
—*Byron.*

"Love's holy flame forever burneth;
From heaven it came, to heaven returneth."
—*Southey.*

"'Tis hard to say, if greater want of skill
Appear in writing or in judging ill.
—*Pope.*

ST. LOUIS:
W. S. BRYAN, *PUBLISHER*,
1880.

RYAN, JACKS & CO., PRINTERS.

TO

## MY MOTHER,

THESE POEMS

ARE

## AFFECTIONATELY DEDICATED.

# CONTENTS.

# LOVE OR FAME.

---

## PART I.

## GIRLHOOD.

GIRLHOOD, the dearest time of joy and love,
The sunny spring of gladness and of peace,
The time that joins its links with heaven above,
And all that's pure below; a running ease
Of careless thought beguiles the murmuring stream
Of girlish life, and as some sweet, vague dream,
The fleeting days go by; fair womanhood
Comes oft to lure the girlish feet away,
But by the brooklet still they love to stray,
Nor long to seek the world's engulfing flood.

HILDA—a name that seems to stand alone—
So strong, so clear its sharply echoing tone;
And yet a name that holds a weirdlike grace,
Withal like some strange, haunting, beauteous face;

A woman's name, by woman's truth made dear,
That leans upon itself and knows no fear,
And yet a name a shrinking girl might wear,
With girlish ease, devoid of thought and care.
And she is worthy of this name so true—-
This girl with thoughtful eyes of darkest hue,
This maiden stepping o'er the golden line
That separates the child from woman divine.
Not yet she feels the longing, vague unrest
That ever fills the woman's throbbing breast,
But with a childlike questioning after truth,
She lingers yet amid the dreams of youth.

And now upon the bounding ocean's shore
She stands where creep the wavelets more and more,
Until at last the rocky ledge they meet,
And break in foam around her lingering feet.
Her eyes glance downward in a careless way,
As though she loved their soft caressing play,
And fain would stand and muse forever there,
Lulled by their murmuring sound.

              Placid and fair
The ocean lies before her dreamy eyes,
Stretched forth in beauty 'neath the sunny skies,
And through the clouds' far lifting, sheeny mist
She sees the pale blue skies by sunlight kissed.
Enraptured by the calm and holy scene,

She stands a creature pure and glad; serene,
Her eyes glance heavenward and a roseate shade
Plays o'er her Hebe features—perfect made.

A child of nature. she has never known
The arts and wiles which worldlier spirits own;
She loves the ocean's ever changing play,
When round her form is flung its dashing spray,
And oft she laughs in wildest, merriest glee
When folded close within its billows free.

She loves the wildwood's green and leafy maze,
Within whose foliage hide the sun's bright rays;
And like a child she hoards the bright-eyed flowers,
Companions of so many happy hours.
With loving heart she greets each form of earth,
To which God's kindly hand has given birth.
But better far than all, she loves to roam
Far on the cliff's lone height, and there at eve
To watch the dark ships as they wander home.
Strange dreams in this calm hour her fancies weave,
So quaint and odd, they seem but shadowy rays,
Caught from the sunset's deep, mysterious haze.

Lo! now she stands like some pale statue fair,
With eyes cast down and careless falling hair;
She vaguely dreams of things that are to be,
A woman's future, noble, fresh and free;

And o'er her face youth's crimson colors flow,
As with a beating heart she thinks she'll give
Her life to one true heart, and with a glow
Of pride she vows her future life to live
So good and true that all her days shall seem
But the fulfilment of his heart's proud dream.

Yet soon she trembles with some unknown thought,
A vague and restless longing fills her breast,
And with a passionate fear her mind is wrought.
She cannot cast away the strange unrest;
With hands clasped close in attitude of prayer
She stands, her pleading face so young and fair,
Is turned unto the skies, but no, not here
Will God speak all unto her listening ear;
Too soon in dark, deep strife upon this shore
Her soul will yield its peace forevermore.

And then she hurries home with flying feet,
The faces of that humble home to meet:
For there in peace her dear old parents dwell,
That simple twain who love this maid so well
They fain would keep her with them ever there,
A thoughtless child, free from all grief and care.
But ah! they cannot understand the heart.
Which turns from all their loving ways apart,
And dwells within a region of its own.
Within that home she seems to stand alone,

## GIRLHOOD.

While all unseen the forces gather, day
By day, that o'er her life shall hold their sway;
And like a fragile flower before the storm,
She bows her head and bends her slender form,
For even like the floweret she must stand
And brave the tempest, for 'tis God's command.

And like to her how many a girl has stood
Upon the unknown brink of womanhood
And sought in vain for guiding hand and power;
But unlike her in that dread trial hour,
They've lost their faith. for Hilda's trusting mind,
E'en though it stood alone, had so much strength,
And faith that to life's problem she could find
Solution strange and subtle; even though at length
She might complain and grieve o'er all the wasted past.
Oh! life is dark and full of unseen care,
And better were it if all girls thus fair
And young were truly understood at last.
For every girl some time will feel the need
Of loving hearts to strengthen and to lead,
When first are opened to her wondering eyes
The world's fair fields and seeming paradise.
She only sees the beauty—hears the song,
Knows not the hidden snares, nor dreams of wrong.
'Tis woman's happiest time, and yet 'tis true
A sombre tinge may mar its brightest hue.
For girlhood too will have its doubts and fears,

Will lose the past and long for coming years,
And sad indeed when youth is left alone
To face the coming future all unknown.
The eyes see not that should be strong and keen;
While powerless, weak girlhood stands between
The tides of life, and though its aims are high,
How often will they fail!

            Where dangers lie
Poor Hilda stands and knows it not, the dream
Of life to her is bright, youth's sunny gleam
Shines over all in tender, softened light,
And swiftly do the moments wing their flight.
But yet so sensitive her shrinking soul,
That o'er her life sometimes great shadows roll,
Like angry clouds; upon a wild dark shore
She stands, alone and weak, while more and more
The unknown forces grow and cast their blight,
Till all the past is lost in one dark night;
Unto the woman's lot her life is cast,
And like a dream the girlish days drift past.

# PART II.

## THE STORM.

ONE eve she stood upon a lonely lea
'And watched the deep'ning shadows grim
That threw their forms athwart the restless sea,
Making the radiance of the West grow dim.
A glorious canopy appeared to rest
O'er changing sky and distant rocky caves.
While o'er some weary sea-bird's pure white breast,
A bright glow spread when dipping in the waves,
Her tired form found therein coolness ; peace
Supremely reigned, and under Silence's wings
Vanished afar and near the waves' wide rings ;
Still grander grew the heavy golden skies,
With gorgeous hues and airy snow-white fleece,
And dreamier grew the maiden's watching eyes,
As through and through her trembling soul and frame,
The thrill of nature's beauty softly came :
And while her eyes with love and rapture filled,
Of all that weird and strangely splendid scene,
All other thoughts within her soul were stilled.
While o'er her head fair spirits seemed to lean.

Around her grew a stillness unto death,
The waves their ever restless motion stayed;
All living nature seemed to hold its breath,
As if by some stupendous power o'erweighed;
And right athwart the sunset's fading glow,
A great black cloud, like some huge monstrous thing,
Threw round and round the sun's last dipping ring
The impress of its shadow drooping low;
And lower, lower fell that mighty cloud,
With menacing shape as in defiance proud.
Until at last all sky and earth and sea
Seemed filled with shadows from its darkening wings—
That dreadful spell cast over waves once free,
Hushed into silence deep all living things.

And still the maiden's watching, eager eyes
Were fixed unmoved on black'ning sea and skies;
So motionless she stood with hands clasped close
And heart-beats growing few and fainter all this time,
That e'en it seemed as though the life-blood froze
Within her veins, like streams in frigid clime!
To-night she'd seen strange visions in the clouds,
Of cities great and busy murmuring crowds,
That called her on to some far different life,
'Mid active minds and noisy, changing strife.
With beating heart she saw the clouds unfold,
Within their depths there gleamed a crown of gold.

Too soon the scene had faded from the skies,
While o'er the earth the threat'ning cloud had spread
That rudely thrust itself before her eyes
And filled her with an overpowering dread;
Yet still she stood with proud, unbending form,
Though all the world seemed near some awful doom.
That dreary silence but foretold the storm
That soon would rage within the night's dark gloom;
A deathly hush o'er waiting land and sea,
And then with one loud clap the storm cloud burst.

Behold! the elements again set free,
As if with fearful spell they'd long been curst,
Now vented all the power of stifled birth
Upon the luckless unoffending earth.
The waves around the cliff's low base sprang high
And madly dashed their spray in furious rage ;
The maid, howe'er, looked down with scornful eye,
As if she could their mighty power assuage.
She gloried in that strange, terrific storm,
The lightning's glare and hurried thunder peal
Awakened in her slight and girlish form
A hidden might that bade her trembling kneel
Upon that lonely, wave-encircled height
And pledge her life to fame, that she might win
The glory of the world's enthroning light,
Then give it back to God all freed from sin.
Long, long she knelt, her soul in prayer thrown,

Unheeding still the lightning's lurid glare ;
For what were raging storms and nature's moan
To that mad strife within her bosom fair !

At last the lightnings ceased, the winds grew still;
All powers recognized God's mightier will ;
Old ocean, like a child with passion spent,
Lay gently sobbing in its rocky bed ;
Anon it sighed and to the dark waves lent,
A sad, sweet song ; the storm indeed was dead.
Along the sable robes that veiled the sky,
The red stars glowed, yet paled each tiny fire
Before the yellow moon, who, throned on high,
Hung on her crescent bow a golden lyre.

From Hilda, too, the stormy grief had fled,
And with a strange, deep peace inspired, she rose
From off the rocks and lifted up her head.
The moon smiled on her upturned face, and close
Beneath her feet the waves swept to and fro.
A smile as that which lit the tide below,
Then dawned upon her lips, for God her prayer
Had heard ; that harp of gold—these skies now fair,
Seemed but the emblem that her soul's dark strife
Should lead her soon unto a nobler life.

Beyond her, on the ledge, a dark form stood,
Regarding her with wistful, wondering eyes ;

He seemed the type of all that's true and good
In man; down from the starry, moonlit skies
The radiance fell and crowned his youthful head,
While on his brow a dim, vague majesty
Seemed shadowed forth.   Yet restless as the sea
His eyes that Hilda's fair young face had read.

With beating heart he'd watched her kneeling there
Upon the rocks; had listened to her prayer
In silence wondering; so strange it seemed
To see her there amid the storm, but still
He stood and powerless; a gladdening thrill
Ran through his veins to see that form alone,
And o'er his noble, Godlike face there gleamed
A pride to think this maid was all his own.
He loved—and love our hearts can ne'er repress—
In truth he gazed upon that face and form
As though upon her head each wet and gleaming tress
Were more than all the phantoms of the storm.
He loved as even the sun must love the flowers
That shyly glance to him 'neath leafy bowers,
Or as the river with its strong deep tide
Must love the willows nestling by its side.

She stood as one within a waking dream,
Nor looked upon the earth, nor on the sky;
But only far at sea whose amber gleam
Was as the light that in fair gems doth lie.

Entranced she stood—the mocking visions came—
But see ! she starts ; upon the air her name
Steals like a whisper of the wave's low song,
Borne by the zephyrs of the night along.
She turns—beside her on the rocks he stands
With questioning eyes and eager, outstretched hands ;
She smiles, then starts back with a startled look,
As some wild fawn within its sheltered nook.

" Fair Hilda, tell me why with reckless feet
  You braved the elements and dared to kneel
  Here in the angry storm—it was not meet
  That all this night's wild tempest you should feel."

She looked at him with almost haughty air,
To think that to reprove her he should dare ;
Then fearlessly as some undaunted child
She met his eyes that searched her own for truth.
She who had scorned the tempest dark and wild,
Feared not the chidings of his hasty youth.
And undismayed she moved to where he stood,
With blushing, beauteous charms of maidenhood,
And there with rapt eyes looking up to him,
She told him of those visions never dim ;
Of that wild spirit born amid the storm
Whose restless strength had swayed her fragile form.
Before his own she laid her very soul,
That he might there its inmost thoughts unroll.

Her pleading voice grew stronger with each word,
Until enthralled and hushed his spirit heard.
Upright she stood in girlish, thrilling grace,
The glancing moonlight falling o'er her face;
It seemed as though some heavenly, unknown power
Had come to her within that strange, short hour,
To make the listener feel the truth divine
That lingered in her words and true design.

Her rich young voice flowed on and on,
In silvery cadence earnest, clear and strong,
And still he stood with bowed head 'neath the skies
Bound by the fascination of her eyes
And winning voice—and manly though he stood,
He humbly bowed before that womanhood
Which seemed with conscious might to grasp the power
Of fame, the world's alluring, phantom flower.
Amazed he stood, before her words struck dumb;
And startled gazed—the maid he loved had come
This night to teach him that her woman's soul
Had dared to seek, than his, a higher goal.

At last each thought was told; with eager eyes
That glowed with fire, as stars throughout the night,
She waited as some birdling ere it flies,
Awaits to poise itself for stronger flight.

But he, when that dear voice had ceased to flow,

1

Awoke as if from some entrancing spell;
He knew not what to say, but to and fro,
He paced awhile with restless step ; too well
He knew her dauntless will, her fearless heart;
He dared not say her dreams, her plans were naught,
And yet to lose her—quickly came the thought—
It roused him with a sudden mad'ning start.

"Oh ! Hilda, unto me these things do seem
But burning traces of some ill-starred dream ;
I grieve that e'er thy soul should long to claim
The thorny diadem of worldly fame.
Life's mystery to thee is yet unknown ;
Why dost thou seek its misery to own ?
With all a woman's power thou this night
Hast led me on by th' fascinating light
Of thy dear eyes and voice, till almost blind
To reason, I allowed my wandering mind
To follow as a willing captive thine ;
I listened with a will not wholly mine.
But now when freed from th' witchery of thy voice
I see no wisdom in thy new made choice.
Thou art a woman pure, whose noble heart
Would fain do, in this world, its earnest part ;
But Hilda, with a girl's weak, erring hand,
Thy hopes are builded on the treacherous sand.
Give up this dream that in thy mind now lies
And be again my Hilda, glad and wise."

"No, no," the dark eyes flash with sudden fire,
"Of this bright dream I know I ne'er shall tire;
The busy world has called me, I will go
And take my station, be it high or low."
"Dear Hilda," then his voice grew low and sweet,
"I love thee; and my love has not been brief.
When thou wert young I led thy wand'ring feet,
And ever guarded thee from pain and grief.
Through all my life thou wert its hope and pride,
But now you turn from that true life aside,
And long to wander as a wilful child,
In other paths, by luring dreams beguiled.
Not so my love for thee; though e'en the sun
Should disappear, his race of glory run,
And stars like lost souls wand'ring through the sky,
Should vanish as that sun; though worlds should die,
And all the purple clouds should come at eve
And for the earth a robe of mourning weave,
While to the very skies the seas should roll
In waves of grief to sweep the heavens' scroll,
It could not change my smallest thought of thee;
I count a man as naught if he's not free,
Yet willingly for thy dear sake I'd live
Where all the world my freedom could not give,
If that I knew could save thee from one tear.
Then wherefore take from me thy presence dear?
If thou would'st wear a crown, why leave this scene?
But stay! I'll crown thee as my love—my queen."

She sadly drew away with troubled mien,
O'er bending face a heightened color spread,
" You cannot understand me yet," she said,
" I'd rather be a *woman* than a *queen.*"
Then wistfully she looked out on the sea,
" I have a gift that God has given me,
I'd use it that the world should better grow;
I long for fame because I then should know
My power was felt and recognized—but stay,
My words are vain, you sadly turn away."

" Choose, Hilda," then once more he proudly cried;
Upon his face there gleamed a passionate pride;
" Between this love that I now offer thee
And that vain fame as faithless as the sea.
I give thee deepest love that man can feel,
Before thine own my heart in truth doth kneel.
Beware how you do mock your early love,
Lest it should die as some poor tortured dove;
If once 'tis dead your woman's heart may grieve
Itself to death; return it never will,
And like the sun, a shadow it may leave
Whose glory, dead and gone, will haunt you still."

Her eyes were filled with grief, her head bent low,
Upon the shore the waves crept to and fro,
Their moan was vaguely echoed in her breast
That vainly struggled with its great unrest.

Her heart was throbbing with the heavy pain
His words had caused; on each fair cheek a stain
Of crimson lay, as that which softly falls
From setting sun on gleaming marble walls.
It rose unto a glow, then died away
In fitful gleams; on drooping eyelids lay
A weight, yet 'neath those heavy veils of snow
The dark eyes quivered with a restless glow.

She could not speak, mute as the rocks that stand
In stony silence now and evermore,
She stood, while stars looked down from heaven's shore
And pitied her.   Unto his proud command
Her heart had not yet dared to make reply,
Lest in those words a deeper pain should lie.

Impatient grown, he paces to and fro
Upon the rocks, then on the tide below,
Looks down with troubled frowns and stifled sighs.
As quick as light across the calm, clear skies,
A meteor flashes down, a dazzling sight,
Then dies, and all the heavens seem as before.
" Look, Hilda, look! so dies this lamp of night
That once was placed upon God's starry floor
To give us light, while yet doth gleam each star
That calmly moves within its own allotted space.
Take warning, Hilda, fly not from thy place,
Nor seek to wander from thy realm too far,

Lest in a trackless waste thy soul shall stray,
And as this meteor, flash and fade away,
While all unmoved the world's calm eyes shall gaze,
Nor give one tear unto thy shortened days."

Back from her face the waves of crimson rolled,
And left it pale as death; as flowers unfold
Their dewy depths, to him her liquid eyes
Were gently raised: " Within that symbol lies
Perhaps a truth," she says, " I dare not say,
Yet, Adrian, it cannot matter now,
Determined is my heart; upon my brow
A crown will rest that will not fade away.
Oh ! seek not in my sorely troubled breast
To rouse again its strength of dark unrest;
For better were my heart in torture wrung
Than linger here and leave its song unsung."

With sad, sad eyes he looked into her face,
Then turned aside with grand, unconscious grace,
And bravely stifled every wayward sigh,
Though in his voice his sorrow still did lie.
" Then as the sea that looks up to some star,
Reflecting its bright beauty from afar,
Thus shall I ever look on thy dear face
And from afar behold thy winning grace.
And as the star's light in the deep blue sea
Still mirrored in my life thy soul shall be.

Even as the ocean hears the star's glad song
Above its own sad, plaintive melody,
So to my heart thy music shall belong
And in my saddest hours will gladden me.
I give thee to that mocking world so vain,
Although it gives me much and weary pain,
And may its ruthless hand be laid on thee
With lighter touch than it has given me.
Remember, if thy spirit should grow weak,
To thee my aid will come if thou'lt but speak
And tell me if within thy troubled breast
A longing comes for loving care and rest.
For even now I love thee none the less
Because thou lov'st not me ; each waving tress
Upon thy brow is still as dear to me
As sunlight to each flower and budding tree.
One look into those eyes I love so well,
And then, dear one—a sad, a last farewell."

With that he caught her small and trembling hand ;
With simple royal grace and gesture grand,
He pressed it to his lips, then let it fall ;—
His dream of love had passed beyond recall.

That touch awakened all her woman's love,
Her heart responded to his silent cry ;
As flowers love the strong, brave sun above,
She loved this man nor ever questioned why.

Before this night no doubts had come between
To mar its trust or stir its depths serene.
Oh! blessed is that love and faith indeed,
Which knows no doubt but only feels its need;
That unsought love which comes and fills the breast
Because we cannot help—that is the best.

With soft caressing touch unto his own
She pressed her hand, then backward swept the hair
Whose shining wealth around her form was thrown;
Her darkened eyes with pleading, troubled air
Looked up into his own; she seemed a child
Beside his strength, yet through his form a shiver
Ran, and to his lips there came a painful quiver,
That told too well the stormy passion wild
This childlike girl had wakened in this hour.
Its might swept o'er his soul with fearful power—
He dared not move—a silence strange and deep
Fell o'er them both, as some half-waking sleep.

To lose her! ah! the fearful, madd'ning thought,
Unto a wilder grief his soul it wrought;
With desperate pride he wrestled with his pain
Lest she should see it in his face again.
But ah! what slender chain of love is this
That can be broken with a last warm kiss!

With longing eyes she stood there by his side,

Her looks fixed on the ocean's tireless tide,
Then gazed down on the robes that swept her feet;
His searching eyes she dared not, could not meet;
And why? within her own the dark tears stood,
True signs of weak and loving womanhood.

At last she put aside her love's young dream,
And all the brighter did its glory seem
Because it must be banished from her heart.
They stood so near, and yet how far apart—
A gulf had come between them, vast and wide,
A gulf made by her longing, restless pride.

With low and trembling voice at last she said,
With sadly falling tears and bended head:

"Oh! Adrian, my faint heart fain would dwell
Forever here beneath thy love's dear spell;
But ah! beyond the height where breaks the day,
There lives a charm that calls my soul away.
Afar the mountains glow in pale, blue mist,
By fleecy clouds and summer sunshine kissed.
And see! beyond them all I long to be,
Beyond this shore, beyond the trackless sea.
Ah! this is why, dear Adrian, we must part,
Although it rends my grieving, restless heart;
Forgive me if to-night I've caused thee pain—
If grief be thine, forgive me once again.

Farewell! when from thy life my love is fled,
Henceforth to thee let Hilda's name be dead."

And this was all—vague shadows crept around,
The waves sung in his ears their moaning sound;.
He looked in vain for Hilda's dear, sweet face,
Forevermore was lost her loving grace
To him.   In vain he called forth in despair;
His words returned upon the empty air.
Like some pale spirit she had stolen from him
And left him there 'mid shadows dark and grim.

# PART III.

## FAME.

H what is fame ! a flower that dies at eve,
A golden mist that subtle fancies weave,
An unknown star that wise men never see,
An idle dream of things that may not be.
Farewell to peace when once the dreams of fame
Shall stir the soul into a restless flame.
There is no rest by day, no sleep by night;
The eyes are blinded by the dazzling light.
Ah ! woe to him who first espies the star,
It hath the power his life to make or mar.

Amid the sombre draperies of the sky,
The faintly-gleaming stars half-hidden lie;
Upon Night's bending head a hood of snow
Seems weighing it unto the earth below;
With gentle frowns she shakes her sable hair
And sends the snow-flakes whirling through the air.
And soon a soft, thick mantle, pure and white,
Gives to the earth a new and holy light.
While with a thousand lamps the city glows
As if encircled with a diadem;
Each lamp transformed into a sparkling gem,

That o'er the earth its flickering splendor throws.
Paris, that brilliant city, gleams to-night
With glittering lights that hide her ghastly woes;
In mockery she's robed in bridal white.
Though in her heart a tide of crimson flows.

The city is aglow with wealth and pride;
A gilded hall is thronged from side to side
With fashion's train of beauteous dames, who smile
And gaily, archly chat the happy while
With gallant men who smile on them again.
All seems forgotten—want and weary pain
That fill the earth with all their drear distress;
Yet many a heart beneath the silken dress
Of its fair wearer hides its weariness
'Neath such bright smiles that none would ever guess
What lies concealed; and handsome, manly eyes
In which the hidden lovelight dreaming lies,
Are telling o'er in silent language sweet,
The love which lips and tongue would fain repeat.
Rich jewels gleam and proud eyes quickly glance,
And costly robes each womanly charm enhance.
From tempting coral lips gay laughter flies,
To be reflected o'er in arch, coquettish eyes.

But see! each tongue is hushed within that hall,
From dainty hands gay fans unheeded fall;
While eyes that one glad moment just before

Were bent 'neath love's warm glances to the floor,
Are looking now, forgetting lovers' sighs,
To see the veiling curtain slowly rise :
And breathless waits that glittering, changing throng,
To hear once more their idol's rippling song.

A face divine, a crown of braided hair,
Dark eyes that gleam with proud and passionate air,
A robe of snowy satin sweeping wide,
A brow that shadows forth a noble pride.

And she is here—the queen of song, Arline,
With flashing eyes and proud triumphant mien.
She smiles—she knows her potent power full well;
With silvery song she breaks the golden spell
Of silence—sings until the walls resound
With echoing strains, and all the air around
Grows tremulous with melody ; high
Beyond the very dome it seems to rise
And reach with daring wings the listening skies.
Within her breast a power that cannot die
Seems lifting her beyond the earth ; along
On living waves of fire her glorious song
Of songs seems borne.   Triumphant in this hour,
Her voice reveals a wild and stormy power
Of weird, sad passion that awakes each soul
Into a mad, sweet ecstasy of pain;
Then low the waves of dying music roll

And leave the air in silence once again.

Ah ! conquering song, thou wert not born of earth,
Celestial stars proclaim thy heavenly birth !
And proud Arline, with wondrous, thrilling art,
Has cast thy spell upon each answering heart.
Oh, sing, Arline, and fear not for thy song !
The music of the waves upon the shore,
Is not so grand as that, nor e'en the roar
Of countless oceans swiftly borne along.
Oh ! poets, rave not of your singing seas,
Your rivers with their rippling melodies;
The human voice alone can touch the heart,
And draw it from its lower self apart.
Then sing, Arline, uplift your starry eyes,
Awake the very echoes of the skies,
And rouse to nobler deeds this eager throng ;—
In all the world there's nought so sweet as song.

But hush—in low sad strains the music dies,
Low at her feet a wealth of flowers lies ;
She smiles—the world's bright fame is clearly won,
Along her veins the quickened fires now run ;
Her dark eyes flash—Oh ! fame, thou art divine !
Into her heart, like streams of blood-red wine,
The world's sweet homage flows ; a deepening stain
Of crimson plays upon her face.   Oh ! fame,
Fear not, for she is thine ; within thy flame

Her soul enraptured burns—and love's sad pain
Is all forgotten in this brilliant hour
That proves too well her strange and gifted power.

But see ! still deeper grows the crimson glow
Upon her face, for at her feet a crown
Is thrown of royal roses ; bending down
She sees in star-gemmed flowers of purest snow
The word " Arline " amid the diadem
Of circling red ; and in their midst a gem
That sparkles with a strange intensive light.
She smiles—a smile that rouses all the fire
In one young heart ; with quick and eager flight
His eyes seek hers ; unto her face still higher
The warm blood flows beneath that ling'ring gaze.
Her drooping eyes grow liquid with the rays
Of light within their depths ; the rippling hair,
With burnished hues of brown and amber rare,
Falls o'er the shaded brow ; while sweeping low,
The long, dark lashes hide the deepening glow
In downcast eyes.

Oh ! painter, do not tell
Of silvery streams and shaded, flowery dell,
Nor talk of clouds with faces to the sun,
That hang low down where golden rivers run.
But dare to paint with skillful, cunning art
The secret workings of a woman's heart.

Oh, catch the light that lingers in her eyes—
The passing gleam that o'er the shadow flies;
Then paint for me the secrets of her soul,
That I may read as on some written scroll.
If this you cannot do, then talk no more
Of nature's wealth of deep and mystic lore—
Of waving grass and azure skies; a face
Is worth them all.

                    She stands in sunny grace,
A woman—the fairest picture e'er was wrought;
A poem fresh from God's own living thought.

She turns again, for once more at her feet
A few fair flowers fall—spell-bound she stands,
Then stoops and clasps them all with eager hands;
Blue violets, and roses wild and sweet,
Forget-me-nots and daisies, pure and white—
Oh! dear wild flowers, how came you here this night
To welcome her with shy and modest eyes,
And dewy faces where the sunshine lies.
Caressingly she bends and kisses them
With warm, bright lips—the royal diadem
Is thrown aside for these few welcome flowers,
And all forgotten is the fame—the hours
Of dazzling triumph; like an eager child
She stands and clasps them in her hands; and wild
And restless are her thoughts; oh! mocking fame,

Where is thy victory now! thy burning flame!
On memory's wings she's carried back to where
These same wild flowers perfumed the sunny air.
And once again with childhood's tireless feet,
She wanders on the shore where dark waves beat
And moan.   She bends her head, her eyes are wet
With tears.   Weep not, Arline! your heart may fret
Itself in vain, the world will never care.
Reveal not to these heartless eyes the pain
That clasps your heart, but raise your head again
And let your grand, young voice ring on the air!
See! 'neath your feet the crown of roses lies
All crushed and torn; then lift your proud, dark eyes
Unto this throng once more, and let them see
Within those depths, **a** spirit strong and free.

The fragrant breath of flowers she loves so well
Breathes on her face and wraps her in a spell;
So often may a flower's faint perfume
Bring back the sunny past—the present gloom.

Arline, Arline, the world is at your feet,
Why droop your head. why grow so still and pale?
Are flowers worth tears, does life no joys repeat?
And fame is yours—is this the hour to fail?
And see! those eyes have never left your face,
Those eyes like pansies heavy with the dew;
They seek your own, reflect your royal grace.

Arline, and read your every thought anew.
They wonder at your silence—smile once more,
Thou queenly one, and send that eager heart
Into a rapturous dream.   Upon the floor
There lies his off'ring—turn your steps apart
And crush it not, for he will grieve, Arline,
To see it thus.

                    At last her troubled eyes
Are raised once more, and now a gentle queen
She stands before them all—the shadow dies—
A softened splendor like the night's weird grace
Rests on her brow and faintly-glowing face.
She lifts her head—she sees the eager crowd,
Her blood begins to leap, her eyes grow proud,
Yet still within their liquid depths there lies
A childlike mournfulness, a dread of truth.
Forever fled they are, the dreams of youth,
All broken are the dear and olden ties,
And yet what can it matter to her now
She wears the crown of fame upon her brow.
For these bright laurels that so soon can fade
She's sold her love nor deemed the choice ill made.
Once more upon the silent evening air
Her rich voice ripples like a golden stream
Let loose beneath the sun; a yearning prayer
Within her low-voiced, echoing song doth seem
To lie.   The bounding blood now swiftly flows

Along her veins, and on her face it glows
With warm, bright fires.   With trembling hands are pressed
The flowers against her heart, a dark unrest
Seems in her soul, yet in those glancing eyes
A tender radiance, like faint sunlight lies.
Oh, sing, Arline, and let the echoes die
In deep'ning melody throughout the sky.
Sing on, for hearts are growing pure again
Beneath thy woman's spell; a power divine
You wield to-night to soften and refine.
Faint hearts are growing sad and full of pain,
Proud eyes that have not wept for many years
Are downward cast, and filled with unshed tears.
What though thy heart is in that low, sad song,
They know it not, their souls are borne along
And strangely thrilled by its sweet melody;
They cannot know what thoughts may dwell in thee.
A song may wake the echoes of the soul
And o'er each life the tides of memory roll.

The music dies—she fain would go—but no.
They call her back, again her dark eyes glow
With longing light; once more she stands and sings
The plaintive words whose hidden sorrow rings
Through every heart.   These words her lips repeat;
The crowd move not; they listen at her feet.

When nobler lips than mine shall sing
Of faith and holy love;

And angels round thee closer fling
    Their glory from above ;
Then think thou of my sad, lone song,
    In realms far, far away ;
Though brighter memories round thee throng
    To gild each happy day.

When fond lips with their glad, dear thrill,
    Shall press thine own once more ;
And softly of their own free will
    Shall whisper love's sweet lore;
Then think of one who loved thee well
    In happy days gone by ;
Though round thee glows a golden spell
    That carries thee on high.

Perhaps when each brave life is o'er
    And duties are well done ;
Our hearts shall meet as once of yore
    Beneath a brighter sun.
And there, where life and love are well,
    We never more shall part ;
While will return the olden spell
    To bind us heart to heart.

A parting glance—a glimpse of dreamy eyes,
A fair young face on which a shadow lies ;
And she is gone, the plaintive song is done.

Arline has faded as the setting sun
Fades from the skies, and left no parting trace,
Save memories of her pale and haunting face.

'Tis twelve o'clock, the city lies asleep,
And far above, within the azure deep,
The jeweled stars keep watch.   Down from the skies
A dark veil falls o'er tired, earthly eyes;
Sleep bids us take farewell of care and sin
And seek a nobler, purer life within.
Night watches like a black-robed, silent nun,
When men would sleep, and kindly shades the sun
Till morning comes.   Upon the grim, dark walls
The moon's pale light in softened splendor falls,
And 'neath a mantle of redeeming light
Hides each unsightly stain and time-worn blight;
While unto eyes now old and dim with grief,
Come visions of a childhood glad, though brief,
When mother-love touched from their hearts all care
And left the impress of her teachings there.
As rifts in hanging clouds through which the rays
Of silvery moonlight glance, so o'er each heart
Steal flitting gleams of happy golden days,
When in life's drama sorrow took no part.

Into a stately dwelling dark and old,
A woman glides with troubled, weary air
Her face is pale, her hands are white and cold,

The silken hood falls from her loosened hair ;
She heeds it not, but listlessly she stands,
With thoughtful eyes and tightly folded hands.
At last the maid with noiseless step draws near,
Removes her wraps and in her listening ear
Speaks these few words : "In passing through the crowd
To-night, a man of face and manner proud,
This missive gave to me.   I looked around,—
For one brief moment his face upon me frowned,
Then he was gone, and though I scanned the street,
His form again my glances did not meet."

The lady takes the note with careless hands,
Then turns to where the ling'ring maid still stands
And bids her go.   At last she is alone,
With eyes indifferent, though thoughtful grown,
She looks upon the note.   " Oh woman's heart,
Can you and earthly love ne'er dwell apart?
Why is it though I would not love, love's pain
Must ever follow me.   Are hearts so weak
That they must love though love is all in vain,
And all unworthy is the prize they seek.
Ah, many like to this do I receive,
Couched in such words as do my proud heart grieve;
And oft I wish that woman had no power,
So fleet, it lingers but a tearful hour,
To draw unto herself the love of man,
Whose shallow depths too well her eyes may scan.

## FAME.

Too oft his love with deep and fearful blight
Steals from her woman's life its holiest light.
My heart is not for love, though love is well,
And oft it hath a dear and happy spell.
Wrapped in the cherished mission of my art,
Contentment dwells within my earnest heart.
Within the rippling measures of my song
The choicest treasures of the world belong.
Why seek for more, the world and fame are mine,
Then wherefore love, though love should be divine?"

At last she reads the note; upon her face
A deep indifference lies,—a cold, calm grace;
But suddenly her eyes light up, her hands
Are trembling. with a nervous haste she stands
And glances o'er the page.   What can this be,
Arline, that brings such new-found pain to thee?
At first her eyes are filled with unshed tears,
Brought back by memories of other years;
Anon, her mind by wondering fear is wrought
Awakened by some new unwelcome thought.

Ah! these the words that stir her heart and soul,
And write new truths on life's unwritten scroll.

" Arline, from all the world thou fame hast won,
A crown thou wear'st that fades not with the sun;
Yet chide me not, if now unto thy ear

I speak such words as thou may'st grieve to hear,
For I shall give thee tidings from the shore
Which knows thy face and welcome step no more.

" The two beloved ones left alone, each day,
Grieved more and more until in peace at last
The bounding line of life was safely past,
And all their sorrow then was put away.
They pined in vain for that dear birdling flown,
Who, with swift wings had left them there alone.
Yet oft in gentle tones they spoke of thee
And longed thy fair, young face once more to see.
Unto our far-off shore there sometimes came
Faint rumors of thy longed-for, new-found fame.
This gave them joy indeed, yet more of pain.
For thus they knew their hopes were all in vain.
Allured unto the world was thy young heart ;—
The gay, bright world in which they had no part.

" But, ere thy mother's eyes were closed in sleep,
She gave to me a secret strange to keep ;
'Twas this. that though they called thee daughter, child,
No blood of theirs flowed in thy veins, thy race
Was of a noble kind, to splendor born ;
An ancestry who wore a kingly grace,
The traces of a lineage undefiled.
Upon thy brow their dauntless pride is worn—
But stay, thy mother, child, though strangely fair,

Was but a singer whose voice of wondrous power
Thine own is like, a voice that filled the air
With strange, sweet sounds, and oft, in many an hour,
Enchantment threw o'er all the eager throng
Who came to hear.   Enthralled by her glad song
One young heart pined ; low at her feet he laid
The glory of his life that she might wear
His crown of love.   His wife she soon was made ;
They lived awhile a happy, loving pair,
Until thou show'dst thy tiny, smiling face.
And then thy mother died that thou might'st live.
He grieved as only strong, brave men can grieve
For what is lost.   Then wandered off a pace
To seek new life in lands across the sea ;
He left thee here, thy life was wild and free.
Long years ago came tidings of his death,
Borne sadly on the wind's faint whispering breath.   '
He was a peer, the last of all his race,
His Saxon strength is written on thy face.
Yet in thy veins thy mother's Southern blood
Is bounding with its warm, impetuous flood.
Enough ; my words are wandering ; a will
He left that may thy heart with gladness fill,
Thy girlish right he recognized at last
And left for thee his rich and vast estate.
Into the world's deep tide thy life is cast,
Yet thou art still the mistress of thy fate.
If thou would'st wear thy birthright's name and power

Speak but the word and claim thy rightful dower."

And this is all, her head is bending low,
From shaded eyes the tears unbidden flow.
Across her face the dark'ning shadows fly
That tell too well the thoughts that hidden lie.

"Oh, God! where is the joy that honor brings,
Where is the spell a golden glory flings,    .
When one short hour, like this, of passing pain,
Can prove the brightest hopes of life are vain ?
I fondly dreamed that fame's short, fleeting power,
Could satisfy my heart in every hour.
Then wherefore is this pain, these sudden tears,
That fall like rain upon the last few years,
And wash their glory out ?   What joy is mine,
When two dear hearts that loved me as their own,
Have gone and left me, saddened and alone !
Sweet mother, had I heard that voice of thine
My life had not been thus.   Can fame, though dear,
Replace that loss or save me from one tear ?
And can it fill my heart through all the years—
Oh, God! be kind, my heart is full of fears."

A passionate misery o'er her fair face swept,
It awakened all the fires that long had slept.
She threw the missive down, and paced the floor
With restless steps, then suddenly stood still.

Unto her heart there came a dreadful thrill
Of grief as she had never felt before;
Her face grew pale as death, her lips were white,
And then she cried, " Oh! Father, pity me,
For I am grieved and full of doubt to-night.
I sink as one into a dark and lonely sea
Where ships are not, so desolate it seems.
Oh! can it be my aim in life is wrong,
Are hearts no better when they hear my song!
My visions fair,—Oh! are they then but dreams,
That do no good, but only lure my heart
From woman's truer paths in life apart?

" Oh! Adrian, had'st thou then the better thought,
And have I but a web of sorrow wrought?
Do all our hopes but lead to care and pain,
Has life no sunshine, only clouds and rain?
Has woman no power to rouse to nobler deeds
The heart of man, and fill his higher needs!
Oh. God! in heaven, guide thy child to-night,
Upon my longings shed thy holiest light.
Oh! mother, with thy tender, loving eyes,
Look down upon me from the starlit skies."

Upon her knees she sinks upon the floor
As one upon a wild and stormy shore;
Her face against the velvet cushion pressed
With hands clasped tightly to her throbbing breast.

Her robes of satin sweep the floor; her hair
Unloosened, falls low down, a golden snare
Of wondrous lights and shades; and pale and cold
Her face gleams 'neath that veil of brown and gold.

Her breath comes quick, she battles with the storm
That gathers in her breast and trembling form.
She stills her heart—heeds not its painful throb,
Drives back her longings, stifles every sob;
And bravely through the watches of the night,
She turns her soul to God for help and light.
A prayer breathed low, a struggle long and wild,
Then peace comes near, and like a weary child,
Worn out with grief, Arline lays low her head.
A silence falls, the night is almost fled,
The lamp burns low, the moon with mystic grace
Looks down upon her fair, uplifted face.
She moves not, o'er her dusky, shaded eyes
The lids lay closed, a moonlit splendor lies
Upon her broad, white brow, and cheeks of snow
Are pressed against the crimson velvet's glow
On which her head is lain.

    Oh, ne'er was wrought
A fairer form than thine, Arline, nor thought
Was ever purer than thine own; though wild
And free thy life has ever been, a child
Indeed thou art in ways of sin and wrong.

Within thy eyes and silvery sounding song,
There ever lives a simple, heaven-born truth.
An earnest motive and a girl's fair youth
Are thine, and though thy heart is wrought with fears—
Ah! sacred unto heaven those falling tears—
For these. are more to Him than many a prayer
Said by unholy lips with humble air.
God does not care so much for empty deeds,
If pure the motive that such action feeds.
Then rest, Arline; upon thy pale, young face
There falls the peace of heaven, a lovely grace;
Around thy head the moon's bright, silver rays
. Are not more stainless than thy youthful days.

# PART IV.

## BROKEN LINKS.

OW in the West, a banner floating wide
Of God's own colors hangs in dreamy pride:
A wealth of purple stains and gleams of gold,
A crimson splendor o'er each waving fold;
A heap of gold—a rim of amethyst,
A hanging cloud by glancing sunbeams kissed.
Afar upon the tinted, azure skies
A tiny, cloud of rosy color lies;
A coral on a velvet robe of blue,
A warm, bright wave upon the skies' pale hue.
Oh ! such the sunset sky of Italy,
The land of dreams, of love and melody ;
The country of the passions and the heart,
The mother of th' ideal and of art.

Oh, painter ! still your heart's wild throb and cry,
You cannot paint this sunset though you try ;
The canvas cannot rival Nature's skies,
Before her hand each human effort dies.
Oh ! you must dip your brush in waves of gold
If you would paint for me that amber fold.
Oh ! poet, seize your pen—'tis all in vain,

You cannot paint in words that crimson stain;
Though all your soul in quivering rapture lies,
Your pen brings not those clouds to other eyes.
Though Art has power, still Nature is the queen,
Her hand alone commands this glorious scene.

Back from the shore there stands a villa old
And quaint, upon a sloping flower-wreathed hill,
Along the side there flows a singing rill;
Beyond, the frowning rocks rise clear and bold.
More like a palace is this lonely home,
With marble terraces and princely lands;
Rare paintings fill each high and finished room,
And marble statues made by master hands.
Without, a view of waves, and skies, and flowers;
Within, a dim, luxurious sense of hours,
Of ease and wealth; a spot where one could dwell
Forever 'neath some strange, enchanted spell.

Upon the steps a woman stands—alone,
Her lovely face, a trifle paler grown
Since last we looked upon its haunting grace.
Yet still the same child mouth, the radiant eyes,
The dauntless pride, that time cannot efface.
Before her gazes the earth in beauty lies;
Awhile she stands and gaze on the scene
With dreamy, far-off looks and thoughtful mien.
Then wends her way to where the flowers lie,

She lingers here, she cannot pass them by,
And as she bends to touch each smiling flower,
Her hands seem gifted with a magic power
That draws unto herself their clinging love,
As human tendrils drawn to God above.

At last with ling'ring steps she takes her way
To where great massive rocks lie near the bay;
Upon a rock which seems a resting place,
Just formed by Nature for some tired queen,
She half reclines, and upward lifts her face
To drink in all the glory of the scene.
Low on her cheeks the veiling lashes sweep
That hide the languid fire within her eyes,
Like shadows fall'n on flowers that softly sleep
Beneath Night's falling dews and bending skies.
Her dark brown hair, with gleams of flitting gold,
Her queenly head encircles as a crown;
A wealth of hair whose careless waves enfold
The quivering sunlight, and its rays chain down.

But soon she starts, for even at her side
There stands a youthful form with fearless pride;
At first upon her face a deep surprise,
And then a haughty look within her eyes,
As turning round she views the handsome face
So near her own with careless, easy grace.
"Why come you here?" she says, "why follow me?
Oh! from thy presence can I ne'er be free?"

" Arline !" he tosses back his sunny hair,
  Half kneels before her with a humble air ;
" Forgive me, for the fault indeed is mine
  To love too well, and for thy face to ever pine.
But oh ! Arline, without thee life is naught,
An idle dream, with only longings fraught ;
And once, Arline, you listened to my prayer.
Nor turned away with cold and haughty air."

She looks upon him with a face aglow :
" Why bring back  memories of the long ago ?
  The past is dead, wake not its depths again,
  Lest such remembrance bring thee only pain .
' Tis true that once a careless, heedless child,
Bewildered by the world, by fame beguiled,
I half allowed my heart to hear thy prayer."
" Yes, yes, Arline," he speaks with eager air,
" I know full well your love was mine, and I
  Now claim the hand your heart cannot deny."

" Lorraine, how can you speak such words to me ?
My love was never thine, my heart is free ;
You know full well I was but kind, Lorraine,
When from thy love I fled to save thee pain.
When first I met the world a vision came
So bright—of glorious power and wealth and fame ;
A part of that bright dream your worship seemed,
That you could claim my heart I little dreamed.

3

Yet soon I woke and with an earnest will
I sought thy mind with deeper thoughts to fill.
It mattered not, your heart's bright flame still burned;—
What were your flowers, your jeweled love to me?—
I loved thee not; each one I would have spurned,
Had not my woman's heart been kind to thee.
At last to fly from thee, the season o'er,
I refuge sought upon this lonely shore ;
And though the riches of the world were thine,
They could not win for thee one thought of mine."

His face grows darker with a fiery pride,
His eyes flash forth the love he cannot hide ;
He rises to his feet, across his soul
A passionate fury his will cannot control,
Bursts forth :

           " Arline, you know not what is love !
To tell me this, for by the fates above,
You shall be mine ! See, yonder is my boat,
Upon the waves with me you soon shall float.
Hush ! rouse me not or you shall see
What angry might your scorn has wrought in me."

"Lorraine !" she meets his gaze with fearless eyes,
Though on each cheek a burning crimson lies.
She folds her arms and stands before him there
A womanly woman, pure, and good, and fair.

She says no word, but who can tell the power
An earnest woman wields in such an hour?

He turns away—a silence falls—the night
Is coming on, the sun has taken flight,
Upon the skies a veiling shadow lies.
She moves not—from her face the color dies
And leaves it pale and calm.

          Unto her side
He comes again: "Forgive my hasty pride,
Arline, for me thou art too purely good,
And far above me is thy womanhood."

For answer she extends her jeweled hand,
He takes it with a loving awe, as though
It were a sacred thing, and thus they stand.
At last he speaks: "Arline, before I go
The secrets of thy life I'll tell to thee,
That you may see 'tis not unknown to me.
You say you ne'er have loved—'tis false, before
You sought for fame, upon a wild, dark shore,
You lived and loved"—to Arline's questioning eyes
There came a startled look—a vague surprise—
"The one you loved, Arline, no more loves you,
Although, perchance, you dream that he is true."

Why grow so pale, Arline, why stand so still?

Have you no woman's pride ? no woman's will ?
Why should you care ? the world is yours and fame,
And worldly hearts will love you all the same.
It matters not, you parted long ago,
To meet no more.    Why bend your head so low !
Lorraine is watching you with searching eyes,
Before his gaze your poor heart quivering lies ;
He still speaks on, his words are sure, though slow,
They find the truth he long has sought to know.

Back from her face she sweeps the heavy hair,
And looks up with a proud, unconquered air;
Ah ! few have wills like hers to do or die,
To hide each wound, to still each longing cry.
" Lorraine, the secrets of my life are mine,
You have no right to solve its mystery ;
Why seek to penetrate my heart's design ?
How sensitive a human heart can be,
You do not seem to know nor even care ;
You tell me that you love, yet love is rare
And generous, its truth you ne'er can know,
If thus within the dust you trail it low."

The night has come, the clouds are hanging low,
Their splendor gone, the wind begins to blow,
It shifts the clouds across the gloomy sky,
Now lashed to foam the troubled waters lie.
The sails are hurrying home, the sea bird flies

Around and round with frightened, screaming cries.
From rock to rock across the frowning hill,
And deep within the vale, a muttering sound
Of far-off thunder rolls along the ground,
A herald of the storm, then all is still.

And yet they heed it not, " Arline! Arline! "
. He cries with flashing eyes, " my peerless queen,
I cannot give you up, you must be mine;
You thrill my heart, your beauty is divine.
What matters it though you have loved before,
You cannot love him now, that dream is o'er.
Look up, Arline, within your starry eyes
There lies for me the only paradise;
I care not for the heaven or earth below—
If you are mine, what care I more to know ?
A woman's love can make man what it will,
For love and thee my heart is throbbing still.
Oh! quick, Arline, for see on yonder height
The lightning circles round with flashing light,
It grows so dark—I scarce can see your face,
Give me your hand, I'll lead you to the place
Where waits my boat ; before the storm comes on
We'll reach the farther coast, for I am strong
And young."

His face is close to hers—she starts
And with a shudder shuts her frightened eyes ;
A silence as of death—the storm-cloud parts ;

A sheet of lightning flashes o'er the skies,
It blinds his eyes, then all is dark again.
Where is Arline?　She is not there, in vain
His search—how fierce the storm, how black the night!'
Another lurid flash—what fearful sight
Is this?　Arline upon the ground, her head
Against the rocks, as pallid as the dead.
And look! on one fair temple lies a stain
Of blood, and on her dusky veil of hair,
The crimson moisture too—what cruel pain
The rocks have caused; and yet how pale and fair
She lies, unconscious of the rain and storm.
"Oh, God! what fearful sight is this to see!"
Half frantic he attempts to lift her form
Into his arms—but no, it shall not be,
For suddenly a hand is laid on his
With iron grasp; upon the stormy air
A voice rings out, "To touch her do not dare,
Or you shall pay the penalty of this;
If she is dead 'tis by your hand alone—
One pitying thought your dark soul does not own.
Begone, or here beneath this angry sky,
Upon these rocks one of us two must die.
Ah! think you not, you fair-faced, proud Lorraine,
I know you not; and well I know the pain
You gave Arline; her lovely grace is far
Above you as the highest, holiest star
That decks God's throne; then go and leave her here,.

For sacred as the dead she is to me."
'Tis Adrian—he drops upon one knee
And looks upon her face with dread and fear,
Then tenderly he wipes away the red,
Dark stains, and with a strong, yet tender grace,
Uplifts her to his arms.

             Her marble face
Lies close unto his own—he bends his head
And is he any less the man because one tear
Falls on that wayward face so proud and dear?
What thoughts are his! they parted long ago
To meet again, but how?   Ah! who can know
What bitterness he feels—that slender form
Within his arms.   Beneath the fierce wild storm
He hurries to her stately home, and there
Her followers wait with hushed and frightened air.

Oh! can it be that she is dead, Arline—
The idol of his heart, the world's proud queen?
No, no; it must not be, her white lids move,
She wakes once more to life and song and love.
The pale lips quiver with a sudden pain,
The lashes half unveil the eyes again.

He gives her up, and leaves her to their care—
When she awakes she must not find him there.
Oh! brave, warm heart, your love indeed is true.

You give your all though naught is given you.
True love is like the watching stars of night,
They shine for aye though eyes see not their light.
And Adrian, fear not, God hears your cry,
In His strong hand your fears and sorrows lie.

# PART V.

## LOVE.

AND what is life?—a pleasure and a pain,
A vision of the sun—a day of rain.
And what is love?—a dream, a chain of gold
That turns to iron bands when love is cold.
What matter they?—the visions of our youth,
Through years of sorrow we must pass to truth.
A woman's life is full of longing days,
Her heart is not content to live on praise;
She must have more; a woman measures life
By length of love, a man by deeds and strife.

ARLINE! once more we greet thy sunny face.
Once more behold thy noble, earnest grace;
But ah, how changed! the hopes of youth are dead;
Life's dark unrest has bowed thy proud young head,
And fame the mocking vision of thy youth,
Has led thee from the paths of peace and truth.

With longing eyes Arline is standing now,
Her arms are folded with a weary air;
The same deep pride is written on her brow,
As once was there of old; her gold-brown hair

Is gathered back in careless waves of light
That hide a scar—the memory of one night.
Her eyes look down, her dark robes sweep the floor—
She starts, for some one passes through the door;
She glances up—recoils with haughty pride,
Which all her self-possession cannot hide;
Then with a look of pity on her face
She meets Lorraine with kind, forgiving grace.

"Arline, I would that I had died indeed
Before I gave thee pain, my heart has need
Of thy forgiveness, else I cannot live,
I crave the boon that only thou canst give."

" Lorraine, the highest graces of a woman's heart
Are purity and truth, no cunning art
Can e'er replace these gifts; 'gainst sin and wrong
They are her surest safe-guards, and her guide
In life. With these she conquers man's dark pride
And wins the tributes that to Heaven belong.
To womanhood belongs forgiveness too,
And therefore is my pardon given you."

With humbled pride he bowed his proud young head,
Then looking in her face he gently said:
" 'Tis nobly given; if women were all like thee,
Arline, how many truer men would be
Within this world; for man will ever go

Where woman leads.   And on this earth below
The grandest masterpiece of Nature's art
Must ever be a woman's sinless heart.
For thee, Arline, the passion of my life is dead ;
The feverish dream is o'er, and in its stead,
There comes a reverence for all thy kind,
And thou, the noblest ideal of my mind.
And now I could not offer thee my love,
For like some pure and upward-soaring dove,
I see thee fly beyond my own weak soul,
To reach a nobler and far higher goal.
Yet, fair Arline, oh, with thy lovely grace,
Uplift my soul unto the realms of thine ;
And with thy tender eyes and pitying face,
Oh lead to worthier deeds this heart of mine ! ' '

" Lorraine, each one must know the price of sin,
    Each erring heart must know what lies within ;
    If we would live aright we must be true
    Unto ourselves ; I cannot govern you ;
    For ah ! we may not read another's mind,
    God puts there thoughts that we may never find.

" We should not judge, for hearts indeed are weak,
    And vain and selfish are the ends we seek ;
    But each temptation, if we do not fall,
    Will tend to make us stronger, all in all.
    Think not thy way is right nor full of power,

For every heart must have its wayward hour;
And though men grieve thee with their outward sin,
Remember nobler thoughts may dwell within.


" And now I thank you for your reverent love,
And yet I feel you place me far above
My own right sphere.   I am a woman weak,
As all proud women are, and soon, too soon,
I feel the world another queen will seek
To wear its crown of fame, and then my noon
Of life will pass as others pass away,
Unto the shadows of the dying day,
And like the foam upon the waves' bright crest,
My life will glide unheeded to its rest ;
Like other hearts forgotten and unknown,
My own will wear itself away alone.
And yet "—and here the dark eyes flashed again—
" The world shall never know its hidden pain,
For late, too late, I feel the world is cold,
It wounds the brow that wears its crown of gold.
Ah! many in the gay and passing crowd
Have thought me cold and even deemed me proud,
When, had they known the truth of that cold pride,
They'd known 'twas but my better thoughts to hide,
When 'mid the bitterness of worldly strife,
I felt for what I'd given my longing life—
To wear upon my head a senseless crown,
On which in scorn my own true self looked down.

Oh, Fame! I chose thee with a girl's weak hand,
And now on life's dark shores alone I stand;
Too late I see the sad mistake I made
When at a worldly shrine my life I laid.
I thought to purify the world by song,
But ah! the world's too full of heedless wrong
For one weak hand to lead it back to truth;
It mocked to scorn my innocence and youth;
To nobler work had I my life but lent,
My restless heart e'en now might be content,
Oh, woman's life was never made for fame,
Her soul is burnt to ashes in its flame."
" You wrong yourself!" he cries at last, " untrue
Your words, for worldly hearts look up to you
And bless your song,—I know, for I am one
Of these, and know the good that you have done.
'Tis true, Arline, an earnest womanhood
Can always do unto the world some good.
One heart in truth has felt your better power,
And that is mine, in this last happy hour;
And have you nobler made even one weak heart,
You've done within this world a worthy part.
And many hearts, Arline, have heard your song
And turned away ashamed from sin and wrong.
No man, however dark his heart, could gaze
Upon a face like yours, where all is pure,
And not regret, oh! bitterly, his days
Of sin.   If every woman would allure

By graces true as thine, there would be less
Of sorrow and of pain, and man would bless
The day that God gave woman to him."

      Her eyes
Are turned to him with eager, glad surprise :
" I thank you for these words," she says, " for true
I feel they are, and in my heart anew
I welcome hope.   And we are friends again,
The past indeed is dead."

      A look of pain
Came in his eyes, yet with a new-born pride
He turned away, that look from her to hide.
" To-night I go, Arline, we meet no more,
Yet in my heart thy image will be there,
To soothe each wayward hour, to lighten care ;
Thy simple teachings have unlocked the door
Of life's best thoughts to me, and if I grow
To better manhood, you have made me so."

Upon her bending head and gentle face
A sunbeam fell and lit with mystic grace
Her dark, uplifted eyes, then quickly fled
To mingle with the sunset's dying red.

A sunny face—a noble womanhood,
A heart's wild passion dead, a new-born pride ;

One moment looking on her face he stood,
Then turned and went forever from her side.


The twilight comes, the first-born child of night,
A warning monitor of time's quick flight;
A dear, enchanted hour, when all are near
We love on earth, and yet an hour of fear
When shadows of the past around us fall
And joy and hope have fled beyond recall.


Within the twilight of the present day,
And shadows of the years now past away,
Arline is standing with a sad, sad air,
Her heart cries out with longing pride and pain.
"Oh, God! what mystery is this of care
And endless doubts; will faith ne'er come again?"
Oh, striving heart, no mind the problem yet
Has solved of life—'tis happier to forget;
When once the mind is roused to questioning thought
With endless misery it may be wrought;
The happiest minds are those that question not—
To live in faith is mankind's fairest lot.


And darker grow the shadows of the night,
She looks upon the sea, the distant height;
Upon the waves the ships go gliding by,
The lonesome clouds throughout the sky
Are wandering with brooding wings, and grim

And shadowy the far-off mountains seem;
Oh! Fame, where is thy joy? oh! love's bright dream,
Where is thy spell? life, like the night, is dim
And sorrowful.

    Low droops her young head fair,
Her whispered words steal on the silent air:
"Oh, what is life, my soul, when love has fled?—
And every one that I have loved is dead,
Save one, and he—oh, must I say it now,—
He loves me not, I dare not claim his vow.
Adrian, too late I prize thee—what is fame
When 'tis not shared with thee! No other name
Can touch me like thine own; but now, indeed,
Where is the love that answers to my need?
I had a dream amid the storm that night,
A vision strange—'mid flashes of the light
Methought I saw your face, your well-known form;
You held me close and safe from rain and storm,
Within the shelter of your arms I lay
And breathed not, lest the dream should pass away;
Oh, Adrian, it seemed as though a tear
Fell from your eyes upon my face, and dear
That mark of pitying love was unto me.
My hair seemed wet with blood—with dreadful pain
My temples throbbed, yet there with love and thee
I felt it not, nor heeded I the rain.
Too soon, howe'er, the vision passed away,
And I was left alone.

"Oh! waves at play,
Mock not my hollow heart with songs of eve,
For olden days I evermore must grieve,
My own sad song forever must be still,
Of empty fame my life has had its fill.
Oh! heart be still, keep back your hungry cry,
Our griefs we all can conquer if we try;
Oh! soul shrink back into thy smallest space,
For thee the heedless world will give no place.
Oh! what is life when only shadows fall!
Oh! what is love, when love is past recall!
My laurel wreath unto the winds I fling,
For worldly praise I never more will sing.
Oh! tears, what do you here—keep back, I say,
Each human life must know a sunless day."

Unto her breast her hands are tightly pressed,
She bravely struggles with the old unrest;
Yet lower droops her form, the lashes sweep
Across her cheeks. Dark memories seem to creep
Upon her heavy heart and weigh it down,
As shadows fall at night o'er vale and town;
And still and white as some pale form of death
She stands, with folded hands and faint drawn breath.

But suddenly through the silence of the room
The one word "Hilda" pierces through the gloom;
A whispered word, yet see! it makes her start,

And sends the life-blood throbbing to her heart.
She turns—her face is stained with crimson o'er,
It dies and leaves her paler than before.
Oh, life is dark, and hearts are weak and wild!
With one faint cry she sees his longing eyes,
His outstretched arms, and as a tired child,
Unto that last, safe refuge quickly flies.

Then presently her head droops low again,
She draws away—there comes a bitter pain.
" Oh, Adrian, my life has all been wrong ;
I am not worthy now your love to claim,
My erring heart is selfish, and to blame,
To sorrow and to grief it should belong.
I left thee with a willful, proud design,
And cared not that a hopeless life was thine.
To give unto thy care, what have I now ?
A worn and wasted life—a broken vow."

" No, no ! look up, Arline, bend not your head;
You wrong yourself—your life is good and true,
And pure the motive that your actions fed ;
Life's highest meed of praise belongs to you;
Few hearts possess your true and earnest thought,
Else would the world with nobler deeds be fraught.
No man could look into your earnest eyes,
And claim that truth in woman never lies,
Nor could he gaze upon that lovely face,

And scorn again a woman's pleading grace.
I wonder not the world has worshipped thee,
For well thy beauty's spell is known to me.
A strain of music can awake the soul,
A kindly grace may touch the hardest heart.
Then weep no more, Arline—you've reached the goal—
The world is better for your sweet-voiced art.
And, Hilda, had thy power not been good,
My love these years could never have withstood."

Her face is turned to his with eager gaze
She drinks in all his words with ecstasy.
"Oh, Adrian, far dearer than the praise
Of all the world those words come now to me ;
Yet tell me, Adrian, is woman's life
Naught but a shadowy dream—a pain—a strife ? "

A grave, sweet smile stole o'er his face, his eyes
Met hers with earnest look, yet half surprise:
"God knows the longings of each human heart,
And each assigns some noble, worthy part,
And they who seek will find; the battle's won
When thought is true, and duty is well done.
From world to world the deeds of man may fly,
Yet in each heart a woman's grace may lie.
Few men may comprehend her longing need—
She lives in thought, he lives in strife and deed.
His boasted deeds may live but for a day

Her purity and truth will live for aye.
The man who claims a woman's hand and heart,
Knows not what boon he craves, what precious thing;
She gives her all—he only gives a part—
She gives her freedom up and crowns him king.
'Tis true she murmurs not,—when love is there
No duty is too great, she feels no care;
'Tis only when that love is cold and dead
She feels the galling chains—the hand of lead.
And therefore do I say to you, Arline,
Of love, and not of fame, she should be queen.
'Tis love that wakes a man to woman's grace;
He first finds heaven when looking in her face,
He sees the trusting soul, the wealth untold
Of noble thoughts that God has written there.
Love binds his heart to hers with chains of gold,
And makes him comprehend the beauty rare
Of womanhood; 'tis this unlocks the door
And shows him truths he ne'er has known before.
Grieve not, Arline; your song has done some good,
An emblem of the true your life has stood.
Your aims were high; your art was truly grand,
Hearts nobler grew, Arline, at your command.
Then do not weep,—Oh, save those precious tears!
The light of heaven shines on the past few years.
And see! the shadows all have fled—the night
Is clear, the stars shine out, the moon's pale light
Is falling on your face; look up and know

The fading of the shadows 'neath the glow
Of night, is but the emblem of the rays
Of happiness that now shall gild your days."

He takes her hand in his—and love's sweet thrill
Runs through her veins, vague dreams her senses fill.
Her face grows childlike in its faith again,
Her heart yields up its wealth of doubt and pain,
Her soft, dark eyes reveal their depths of fire.
" For fame my heart has never more desire,
Were all our planets moons, night could not know
The glory of the day, nor evening show
The splendor of the sun—his light is best.
So, were each heart to worship at my shrine,
All filled with love, it could not equal thine,
For thine is more to me than all the rest.
Then, like the purple pansies, bending low,
That yield unto the sun their royal glow,
Unto the sun-god of my life and years
I'll yield my love, and know no idle fears.
The meteor has flashed across the skies,
Yet in its place a star of beauty lies ;
Adrift into the azure seas above
That star shall sail on wings of hope and love,
While fame, the meteor that mocks the sight,
Shall die upon the earth—a faded light.
And now, for thee alone, my heart shall sing,
Far from my sight my crown of fame I'll fling,

And in its stead, the diadem I'll wear
Of love and womanhood—earth's crown most fair."

Out on the terrace, where the moonlight falls
In silver radiance o'er the time-stained walls,
A man and woman stand—he, strong and fair,
She, lovelier than the flowers that scent the air.
Her eyes are velvety and soft and brown,
Her hair—a shimmering splendor falls low down,
Her dark robes sweep the marble floor; one hand
Is clasped in his; in silence now they stand,
No need of words when silence speaketh more
Than all the wealth of speech, or written lore.

Her eyes are turned to his; no more they grieve;
Oh, who can tell the spell that love doth weave?
The music of the stars, a faint, sweet strain,
Floats down—an echo of their heart's refrain.
Two lives that glow as bright as heaven's own—
Two stars, that in the night have closer grown,
God sets the music in each soul; no hand
But that of *love* the music can command.

The song of life is done—the tale is told,
God grant the chain may count some links of gold.
A woman's life—a man's true love—a song—
What dreams of life may not to these belong!
The weaving of a story, old yet new,

Life's strange, sad mingling of the false and true.
A woman's heart is like a harp of gold,
It yields no music to the touch most bold,
But to the hand that o'er the chords may sweep,
And gently wake the music from its sleep.
An idle dream a woman's life may be,
Yet do not dreams belong to thee and me?
To every life some visions must belong;
Are we to blame that they are sometimes wrong?
True women make true men,—'tis always so;
Yet careless touch may soil the purest snow,
The shadows of the night may hide the sky,
Yet still beyond them all the stars still lie.

# MISCELLANEOUS POEMS.

## TO LONGFELLOW.

HE crown of stars is broken in parts,
Its jewels brighter than the day,
Have one by one been stolen away
To shine in other homes and hearts.
—[*Hanging of the Crane.*

Each poem is a star that shines
   Within your crown of light;
Each jeweled thought—a fadeless gem
   That dims the stars of night.

A flower here and there, so sweet,
   Its fragrance fills the earth,
Is woven in among the gems
   Of proud, immortal birth.

Each wee Forget-me-not hath eyes
   As blue as yonder skies,
To tell the world each song of thine
   Is one that never dies.

The purple pansies stained with gold,
　　The roses royal red,
In softened splendor shadow forth
　　The truths thy life hath said.


Oh would the earth were filled with flowers
　　To crown thee poet-king!
And all the world unto thy feet
　　Its wealth of love could fling.


And would I were one lowly flower
　　That fell beneath thy feet ;
That even in dying I might win
　　One verse of music sweet.


The poet-heart doth hold the power
　　To thrill the hearts of men ;
And though the chain is broken quite
　　It joins the links again.


No hand like thine can sweep the chords,
　　No heart like thine can sing ;
The poet-world is full of song
　　And thou alone art king !


Oh would my eyes could see thy face
　　On which the glory shines !
And would my soul could trace the thought
　　That lies between the lines !

But though my eyes may never see,
  My heart will worship still;
And at the fountain of thy song
  My soul will drink its fill.

Thy crown of stars will never break,
  Its circle is complete;
And yet each heart some gem will keep
  To make its life more sweet.

The following autograph letter was received from the poet:

DEAR MISS SHERRICK:—I am much pleased and touched by the graceful and beautiful tribute you have paid me in your poem. I beg you to accept my best thanks for these kind words, and for the friendly expressions of your letter, which I have left too long unanswered. Pardon the delay, and believe me with great regard,

                    Yours sincerely,
                        HENRY W. LONGFELLOW.

---

## TOWER GROVE.

Oh tell me not of the lands so old
Where the Orient treasures its hills of gold,
And the rivers lie in the sun's bright rays
Forever singing the old world's praise.

Nor proudly boast of the gardens grand
That spring to earth at a king's command;
There are treasures here in the far great West
That rival the hills on the Orient's crest.

Far from the sight of the dusty town
Like a perfect gem in a golden crown,
Lies a beautiful garden vast and fair,
Where the wild birds sing in the evening air,
And the dews fall down in a silent shower
On the fragrant head of each beaming flower;
While far and near o'er the land sun-kissed,
Hangs the roseate veil of the sunset mist.

Under the shade of the western wall
There's a glimmer of roses fair and tall.
And the crimson heart of each royal flower
Gleams purely forth from its leafy bower.
There are things in this world too sweet to last,
But we catch their grace ere the bloom is past,
And the roses that die in the early morn
In the garden of memory anew are born.

The dear little pansies, quaint and fair,
Uplift their heads in the silent air;
And the gleam of the purple tinged with gold
Is as fair as the roses' velvety fold.
There are tropical plants from the Southern seas

Where the flowers sleep in the perfumed breeze;
And the scent of the orange groves fill the air
With a mystical incense rich and rare.

Like waxen buds in a leafy screen
Magnolia blooms float in a sea of green;
And their fragrance falls on the dewy air
Like the breath of the tropics richly rare.
And up from the South in the voiceless night
Steals the scent of the blossoms pure and white,
And one by one as the winds sweep by
They shrink away, from that touch, to die.

There are trees and flowers from every clime
Defying the scope of the poet's rhyme;
There are beautiful lawns where the feet could rest,
Unwilling to wander, forever blest;
There are peaceful nooks where the soul might dwell
Forever lost in a fadeless spell;
But the tomb of the man who is great and wise
Is the loveliest spot in this paradise.

And just to the south is a park so fair
That the children of God love to wander there;
And the emerald green of its winding ways
Is flecked with the gold of the sun's last rays.
There are statues, too, of the good and great,
Who point on forever to Truth's wide gate,

And the bronze and the green and the sun's red gold
Are mingled at eve in a glory untold.

Immortal the name of the man shall be
Who hath given these treasures so fair to see,
And the grace of the flowers he loves so well
The truth of his goodness forever shall tell.
But fairer than all are the deeds of love
That shine in God's temple of grace above;
And Fame on her beautiful shadowless height
Has woven his name in a glory of light.

----

## A SHELL.

Oh, take this shell, this pretty thing
  With tinted waves of pearly red;
Hold close your ear and hear it sing,
  Then tell me what its voice hath said.
    A song of surges deep and strong,
    A song of summer sweet and long,
    A sound of storm and wind and rain,
    A sound of joy—a glad refrain.

O plaything of the idle sea,
  Whence come these changing tints of thine?

Have sunset clouds looked down on thee
  And stained thee with their hues divine?
    Oh, tell the secrets thou must know
    Of clouds above and waves below;
    Oh, whisper of the bending sky
    And ocean caves where jewels lie.

O beauteous sea-shell, tinged with red,
  What dost thou know; what canst thou tell?
Unto what mysteries art thou wed,
    Thou fragile thing, thou pearly shell?
    A whisper of the sounding sea;
    A sweep of surges strong and free;
    A tale of life—a tale of death;
    A warm, bright sun—an icy breath.

Ah, more than this, thou lovely shell,
  Thy years have gathered from the deep!
And, more than this, thy voice can tell
    Of things learned in that ocean sleep.
    A grave within the lonely sea;
    A spot where love can never be;
    A place where tears may never fall;
    A lonely grave—and that is all.

## TWO PICTURES.

A beautiful form and a beautiful face,
A winsome bride and a woman's grace,
So fair and sweet it were heaven indeed
For man to follow where she should lead.

A web of lace and a jewelled hand,
And life is changed by a golden band;
A dream of love and a wealth of gold—
The old new story once more is told.

A wealth of flowers and a robe of snow,
A beauteous woman with cheeks aglow;
A train of satin that sweeps the floor—
And life is altered forevermore.

A beautiful scene on this Christmas eve,
Where all could linger and none could grieve,
A dazzling vision of wealth and pride,
A royal feast and a happy bride.

But turn your steps to the lonely street,
Where fierce winds mutter and wild storms beat;
And come with me to the haunts of woe
Where life is a burden and hopes are low.

Look on this woman, so thin and white;
You close your eyes—'tis a dreadful sight;

But shudder not—she is cold and dead—
And died, oh men! for a *crust of bread.*

So young and hopeless, oh! God above,
With none to comfort and none to love;
A tortured soul and a hungry cry
That rang unheard through the stormy sky.

While, oh ! so near in the gloomy night
Lay rescue and love and warmth and light ;
And oh! so near to the longing eyes,
There gleamed the bright depths of a paradise.

Oh ! look on this picture, thou fair young bride,
For one poor morsel of bread she died ;
One glittering gem from your breast or hair,
Could have saved this woman who lieth there.

One costly spray of your flowers bright
Could have bought the food that she craved this night ;
One drop of love from your boundless store
Her soul could have saved forevermore.

Oh, sadd'ning picture, this Christmas eve,—
For thy sad story the angels grieve ;
To think in this city of wealth and might
A woman perished for *bread*, this night.

## THE QUEEN-ROSE—A SUMMER IDYL.

The sunlight fell with a golden gleam
  On the waves of the rippling rill;
The pansies nodded their purple heads;
  But the proud queen-rose stood still.
She loved the light and she loved the sun,
And the peaceful night when the day was done,
But the faithless sun in his careless way
Had broken her heart on that summer's day.

She had bathed her soul in his warm, sweet rays,
  She had given her life to him;
And her crimson heart—it was his alone—
  Of love it was full to the brim.
But a fairer bud in the garden of love
Had conquered the heart of the king above;
And the proud queen-rose on that summer's day
Had given a love that was thrown away.

The pansies laughed in the summer breeze,
  For they were so happy and free;
And the lilies swayed in the waving grass,
  Like sails on an emerald sea.
But the sun glanced down with a mocking light,
And the heart of the rose stood still at the sight,
For never again with its love for him
Would her crimson heart be filled to the brim.

5

"Ah me!" she sighed, as she drooped her head,
   "How vain is my haughty will;
I sought to mate with the sun above,
   But lo! I am mortal still.
I envy the pansy that nods at my feet,
For though she is lowly, her life is sweet;
And I envy the lily, for she is glad,
And knows not the longings that make me sad."


A maiden sat where the pansies grew,
   In a golden shower of light;
And she heard the words of the sighing rose,
   Borne near in the wind's swift flight.
"Ah, rose!" she cried, "I am like to you;
There's never a heart in this world that's true;
I yielded a love that's thrown away,
And I'm weary of life on this summer's day.


"But listen, my rose, and I'll tell you, sweet,
   The lesson I learned to-day;
There's never a heart in this wide, wide world
   That was born to be thrown away.
The sun may smile as he sails away
In the depths of his azure seas for aye;
But the rose that blooms in the garden of love,
Is as fair as the sun to our God above.

" The smallest flower that slakes her thirst
   In the dews of the early morn,
Is as great as the stars in heaven above,
   The greatest that ever was born.
The love we give on this earth of ours
Is treasured in heaven through all the hours,
And the crimson heart of the proud queen-rose
Is as fair a gem as the earth-land knows."

The queen-rose listened and held her breath
   As the maiden passed her by,
And then, with a grace that was fearless and grand,
   She lifted her face to the sky.
And never again, when the day was done,
Did she long for the love of the golden sun ;
For the lesson she learned on that summer's day
Lay deep in her heart forever and aye.

---

## TWIN LILIES.

Twin lilies in the river floating,
   Two lilies pure and white;
And one is pale and faintly drooping,
   The other glad and bright.

Twin lilies in the silvery waters,
   Two lilies white and frail ;

And one is ever laughing gladly,
   The other, still and pale.

Upon the peaceful gleaming waters,
   They linger side by side ;
And one, her head is drooping sadly ;
   The other glows with pride.

Twin stars are o'er the river beaming,
   Two stars with silvery light ;
And now they look with glances loving
   Upon the lilies white.

Two lilies now are drooping lowly
   Unto the river tide;
While in the wave the stars reflected
   Are floating side by side.

And now the stars are bending slowly
   To kiss the lilies white;
Who e'en their fragrant heads are lifting
   In wonder at the sight.

And one twin lily now is longing
   For light and heaven above ;
And yields unto her star-king's keeping
   Her wealth of life and love.

And as the star-god bends in rapture
  To kiss her pale, white face,
Her soul is wafted into heaven
  Beneath his love and grace.


Twin lilies in the tide were floating,
  With quickly coming breath,
But one is left, with sad tears falling,
  To mourn her sister's death.


Twin stars upon the waves were gleaming;
  Two star-gods pure and bright;
But one is left—that one is fading
  And dying with the night.

———

## MEMORY

A treasured link of shining pearls,
  A by-gone melody,
A shower of tears with smiles between—
  And this is memory.
A thing so light a breath of air
  May waft its life away;
A thing so dark that moments of pain
  Seem like some endless day.

A careless word may wound the heart,
  And quickly it may die;
Yet in the seas of memory
  Forever it will lie.
And someti nes when the tide rolls back
  Its waves of joy and pain,
That careless word, though long forgot,
  Will wound the heart again. ,


The restless seas of memory
  Are vast and deep and wide;
And every deed that we can know
  Sleeps in that tireless tide.
Upon the thoughtless lives of men
  Its waves in mockery roll;
And sweep a might of bitter pain
  Across each human soul.


And few can stand upon the sands
  Beside this boundless sea,
And say with calm unfaltering voice
  " It has no grief for me."
The passing wave may bear away
  Our deeds and words untrue;
Yet surely as the tide comes in
  The wrecks will follow too.

## MOONLIGHT.

Oh, what so subtle as the spell
   The silvery moonlight weaves?
Oh, what so sad and what so glad,
   And what so soon deceives.

A vision of the long ago—
   Long years of pain between;
A mocking dream of happier days—
   A veil of silver sheen.

A passing gleam of falling stars—
   An idle summer's dream;
The sudden waking of a heart—
   Things are not as they seem.

Oh, silver moon, indeed you hold
   The secrets of the heart;
And none can know and none can guess
   The mystery of thy art.

A silvery length of rippling waves,
   A glance from happy eyes;
A strain of music low and sweet—
   The heart in rapture lies.

Yet, ah, how faithless are the vows
   Made 'neath the summer moon;

As changing as the falling rays
    That fade away as soon.

For love is like the subtle spell
    The silver moonlight weaves;
And what so sad and what so glad
    And what so soon deceives?

---

## THE STAR OF YOUTH.

The sun sinks down in the crimson west,
    Oh, a beautiful sun is he;
With his purple robes and his crown of gold
    And his feet dipped in the sea.

Along the shore where the sea-weeds lie
    Like threads of her tangled hair,
Naomi stands in the amber glow
    Of the mystical sunset air.

Her hair is brown, with a yellow tinge
    That rivals the gold of the west;
Her eyes are dark with the velvety glow
    That darkens the pansy's breast.

A star shines out in the purple east,
    Oh, a beautiful star is he!

With his home in the wonderful azure skies,
  And his throne in the deep blue sea.

There are bars of gold in the crimson west
  And jewels on every bar;
Yet Naomi's soul is beyond the sea,
  And her eyes are fixed on the star.

O star that shines in the dusky east,
  Be thou the star of my youth,
And guide my soul through the shadows of earth
  To the shining gates of truth.

There are years that melt in the seas of life
  Like drops in the ocean of time;
And the joys they bring are as soon forgot
  As the words of a careless rhyme.

Be thou the light that shall guide me far
  From the years that vanish as rain,
And lead my soul to the feet of God,
  Even through years of pain.

---

## THE DAY IS DEAD.

  The day is dead,
And evening trails her purple robes
  In fading fires of red.

The day is dead,
And yonder lily welcomes sleep
And nods her weary head.

The day is dead,
And night droops low her sable plumes
To mourn the glory fled.

----

## MY QUEEN.

A fair sweet blossom is born for you,
    A beautiful rose, my queen!
And never was flower so fair as this,
    Oh, never so fair, I ween!
A banner is hung in the western sky
Of colors that flash ere they fade and die;
And the rippling waves where the waters run
Are stained with the gold of the summer sun;
The world is so fair for you, my queen,
    The world is so fair and true;
And the rose that blossoms to-day, my own,
    Is the love that I have for you.

The grasses that spring at your feet, my queen,
    Could whisper all day in your ear;
But I stand dumb at your side, my own,

Stilled by my love's own fear.
Oh, what would you know of my love's sweet will
The heart speaks most when the lips are still;
And the love that is filling my soul to-day
Is the beautiful blossom you throw away.
But I worship you still, my queen, my queen,
    I worship you still, I ween;
For the loveliest blossom on earth I know
    Is my beautiful love, my queen!

---

## THE SONG OF THE BROOK.

Oh, what would you have, you splendid sun,
    With your restless eyes of fire?
And why do you lean o'er the lilies pale?
    What more can your heart desire?

You've crimsoned the rays in the heart of the rose,
    You've drunk up the dewdrops all;
And down in the meadows your golden light
    Has gilded the daisies tall.

The thirsty flowers that grow on the hill
    Have given their lives to you;
And what do you care, you restless sun,
    As you sail through your seas of blue?

Your rays are so warm, like the glances of love,
　　The lily is mad with delight;
And whispers her secret with silent joy,
　　As she kisses my face in the night.

What more can you want, O eager sun?
　　I've given my all to you;
I've counted my treasures and claimed them not,
　　What more can I ever do?

But, eager sun, with your restless rays,
　　Know this, that I love not you;
For the sun that knoweth a world of loves
　　To one can never be true.

———

## NIGHT.

' Tis eventide; the noisy brook is hushed
Or murmurs only as a tired child,
Worn out with play; the tangled weeds lie still
Within the marshy hollow. Quaint and dark
The willows bend above the brooklet's tide,
Reflecting shadowy images therein.
The dark-browed trees, with faces to the sky,
Shut out the light that fades in crimson lines
Along the western sky. And yonder shade

Of purple marks the cloud, the storm-god rides
In moods of angry fire.

The woods are filled
With wild-wood blossoms drinking in the dew.
Their scented breath is sweeter than the maid's
Who stands at eve and drinks in love and hope
From every budding flower.

All day the sun
With fiery breath has held his hot, long reign :
The leaves have quivered 'neath his burning gaze,
And all the flowers have drooped ; yet now the moon,
His pale young bride, awaking from her spell
Of sweet day dreams, arises in the dusky East.
And sweeping back the clouds that dim her crown
Of stars, floods all the world with holy light.

Oh, welcome night ! the flowers love their queen !
Yea, better than their king, for he is fierce
And warm, and drinks the jewelled dew-drops all.
Her hand is cool and soothing ! 'neath its spell
They sink to restful slumber.

Bless'd night !
When all the world's asleep, and thought can fly
On tireless wings from sky to sky, when free
From earthly chains, the soul immortal feels
Its throbbing freedom.

Bless'd night !
When God looks down from every shining star,
And breathes in every dew-gemmed flower, when faith
From her rock-bound temple on the hills
His everlasting glory sings ! Oh, welcome night !
Thy beauty holds the spell that wakes to life
All things immortal.   Crowned be thou with light
Eternal as the sun whose radiance wakes the day.

---

## SOUNDS FROM THE CONVENT.

"Come, pensive nun, devout and pure,
Sober, steadfast and demure."
—[*Milton.*

White-robed nun, I pray thee tell me
Whatsoe'er my life shall be ;
Thou of God art purely chosen,
Ne'er can I be like to thee.

There is sunlight in the shadow
Of the lives we live below ;
There is starlight in the darkness
Of the night of human woe.

Yet-I pray thee, sweet-voiced woman,
Tell me of thy life and thee ;

Can the soul to heaven given
   Yield its secrets unto me ?

Nevermore the earth shall claim thee,
   Only lilies bloom for thee ;
All the world is full of beauty
   That thy eyes may never see.

On the hill the daisies springing,
   Lift their heads to greet the morn ;
Yet thou mayst not pluck the smallest
   Of these blossoms lately born.

Violets may bring no memories
   Unto thee of days gone by ;
Summer eves and joyous mornings—
   In the grave these, too, must die.

Long ago, the roses drooping,
   Crimson blushed and died for thee ;
Yet to-day no more thou know'st them,
   They are lost in Life's dead sea.

Oh, the world is full of beauty !
   Oh, the world is full of love !
Yet the chains that bind thee earthward,
   Link thy soul with Heaven above.

Through the windows creeps the sunlight,
   Rays of gold and restless red;
Covering all the world with glory,
   Sweetly resting on thy head.

Would my life were crowned with sunlight,
   Would my soul was pure as thine!
Then the world no more would know me,
   Earth were Heaven, and Heaven were mine

---

## THE LAKE.

A limpid lake, a diamond gem,
   The moonbeams kissed with light;
And all the stars that heaven knew
   Were mirrored in the night.

How fair the world. how fair the night,
   When lake and river run
Like jeweled streams of fairy land
   Beneath a silver sun.

The lake grew proud and claimed each star
   That lay upon her breast;
"Ah! they are mine," she said; " these gems
   That in my bosom rest.

" And yonder moon, that sails on high,
  Doth shine for me alone ;
Beneath the foam that crests my waves
  Is built her silver throne."

A star-king knelt and kissed the waves
  That swept the shadowed shore ;
" Our moon is queen of heaven," he said,
  " Is queen forevermore.

" A thousand lakes are hers by night,
  A thousand lakes of light ;
A thousand rivers kiss her feet,
  A thousand rivers bright.

" Then be not vain, thou lakelet small,
  The moon is not for thee ;
Her home is in the river wide,
  Her throne is in the sea."

The bright waves swept the silent shore,
  The star-king crept away ;
Yet calm and fair, still unconvinced,
  The lake in silence lay.

The moon, that swept her silvery light
  Far o'er the waters wide,
Belonged to her, and all the stars
  That floated side by side.

6

Ah! silver lake, too well we know
  How like we are to thee ;
A thousand truths are in the world
  That we may never see!

-----

## LIFE.

A dewy flower, bathed in crimson light,
May touch the soul—a pure and beauteous sight ;
A golden river flashing 'neath the sun,
May reach the spot where life's dark waters run ;
Yet, when the sun is gone, the splendor dies,
With drooping head the tender flower lies.
And such is life ; a golden mist of light,
A tangled web that glitters in the sun ;
When shadows come, the glory takes its flight,
The threads are dark and worn, and life is done.
Oh! tears, that chill us like the dews of eve,
Why come unbid—why should we ever grieve ?
Why is it, though life hath its leaves of gold,
The book each day some sorrow must unfold !
What human heart with truth can dare to say
No grief is mine—this is a perfect day ?
Oh! poet, take your harp of gold and sing,
And all the earth with heavenly music fill!
You may do this, yet song can never bring
One sunbeam back, let song be what it will.

Oh! painter, you can catch the glowing light
That tints the skies before the coming night;
With throbbing heart and upward lifted eyes,
You paint the splendor of the purple skies;
Yet tell me, does your genius hold the key
To life's strange secrets and its mystery?
Oh! life is sad, yet sunshine, too, is there;
We cannot tell what spell the years may weave—
Perchance a song that dies upon the air—
Perhaps a shadow that the sun doth leave.

## A MEMORY.

Amid my treasures once I found
    A simple faded flower;
A flower with all its beauty fled,
    The darling of an hour.

With bitterness I gazed awhile,
    Then flung it from my sight;
For with it all came back to me
    The pain and heedless blight.

But, moved with pity and regret
    I took it up again;
For oh, so long and wearily
    In darkness it had lain.

Ah, purple pansy, once I kissed
  Your dewy petals fair;
For then, indeed, I had no thought
  Of earthly pain or care.

Your faded petals now I touch
  With sacred love and awe;
For never will my heart kneel down
  To earthly will or law.

Your velvet beauty still is dear,
  Though faded now you seem;
You drooped and died, yet still you are
  The symbol of my dream.

Sweet, modest flower, tinged with gold,
  A lesson you have said;
Your purple glory, like my love,
  Is faded now, and dead.

———

## THE BABY'S TEAR.

A tiny drop of crystal dew
That fell from baby eyes of blue;
A shining treasure, there it lay
For grandma's love to wipe away.

A tear of sorrow, pure and meek
It graced our darling's dimpled cheek ;
A gem so fair, that angels smiled
And claimed the treasure undefiled.

A sunbeam came with winsome grace
And chased the shadow from her face;
A smile fell trom its wings of light
And baby eyes laughed at the sight.

The wee bright tear was kissed away,
Yet in our hearts its sorrow lay;
For like a shadow came the thought,
With pain and sorrow life is wrought.

Oh, baby heart, what will you do
When life's unrest is given you;
And mother-love no more like this
Each tear can banish with a kiss ?

The love you brought, oh, baby dear,
Is like the sunbeam passing near;
A ray of light—a touch of gold
To keep our hearts from growing old.

Then may thy life grow strong and sweet
With mother-love to guide thy feet;
And may the sunbeams ever chase
Each shadow, darling, from thy face.

## IRENE.

The years are slowly creeping on
    Beneath the summer sun ;
Yet, still in silent love and peace
    Our lives serenely run.
Beyond the mist that veils the coming years
I see no gathering clouds, nor falling tears.

Beside life's river we have stood
    And lingered side by side ;
Where royal roses bloomed and blushed
    And gleamed the lily's pride,
And happily there we've plucked the sweet wild flowers
While heedless passed away the sunny hours.

Irene, thy sunny face is lit
    With all the hope of youth ;
God grant thy heart may never know
    Aught but the purest truth.
Keep in thy soul its faith and trusting love
Until they e'en must bloom in heaven above.

Beside the river still we stay
    And swift the hours fly by ;
While low upon the fragrant banks
    The flowers silent lie.
Yet, far beyond the mist, our longing eyes
Still seek the gleaming walls of paradise.

## UNRECORDED.

The splendors of a southern sun
    Caress the glowing sky;
O'er crested waves, the colors glance
    And gleaming, softly die.
A gentle calm from heaven falls
    And weaves a mystic spell;
A glowing grace that charms the soul—
    Whose glory none can tell.

Oh, warm sweet treasures of a sun
    Of endless fire and love;
Those dying embers are the flames
    From heavenly fires above.
Unto the water's edge they creep
    And bathe the seas in red;
Then die like shadows on the deep
    With glory cold and dead.

A ship—a lone, dark wanderer
    Upon the southern seas,
Speeds like a white-faced messenger
    Before the dying breeze.
Her masts are tipped with amethyst,
    A splendor all untold;
A crimson mantle wraps her round,
    Her sails are made of gold.

The light wind dies—she slowly drifts,
　　Then stops—an idle thing;
While sunset clouds around her prow
　　A dreamy grandeur fling.
And eyes upon her deck look forth
　　With looks of longing pain :
A hundred sunsets they would give
　　Dear home to see again.

But see ! a shadow as of night
　　Spreads o'er the crimson sky;
Like doomed and lifeless forms of earth
　　The clouds in heaven lie.
A silence falls—the ship stands still,
　　A fated thing of earth;
Then like a child of sin and wrong
　　The storm is given birth.

Oh ! struggle well ye gallant crew
　　With storm and wind and wave ;
For there are helpless women here
　　And children, too, to save.
Quick—sailors do your duty well—
　　And man the life-boats, too;
For soon the rocks will strand the ship,
　　And pierce her through and through.

See ! like a woman turned to stone
　　A weeping mother stands ;

Her heart seems like some frozen thing.—
  She wrings her trembling hands ;
Within her arms she holds a child
  With frightened wond'ring, eyes ;
Below—the waters pitiless—
  Above—the angry skies.

Beside her stands a fair young girl
  With eyes that flash and quiver;
They are the only ones still left,
  These three that moan and shiver.
But soon a voice shouts back the words—
  Through all the deaf'ning roar :—
A strong hand grasps the trembling girl,
  " There's room for just one more."

" Stay, stay," she cries with whitened face
  " Why should I fear to die ?
Oh, take this woman by my side,
  Nor stay to question why.
She has a dear one 'mongst your crew,
  She is a mother, too ;
I am alone—I fear not death,
  If this you'll only do."

The sailor grasped the mother's hand,
  She turned and kissed the maid ;
The tears of pity filled her eyes

Yet not one word she said.
The maiden stood with outstretched hands,
  All hope indeed was gone;
And yet she stood with fearless heart,
  Undaunted and alone.


" Oh, God, the heart that knows your love
    Will never need to fear;
A priceless gem lies on my face,
    The mother's grateful tear."
The lightnings swept across the ship,
    The darkness wrapped her round;
Above the thunder of the storm,
    There came no other sound.


The morning broke—the storm had fled,
    The wreck was washed away;
And calmly now as yesterday
    The sea in splendor lay.
The noble heart that throbbed with life
    Lay fathoms deep below:
And what lies buried in that heart
    The waves alone can know.

## BEATRICE CENCI.

O beautiful woman, too well we know
The terrible weight of thy woman's woe,
So great that the world, in its careless way,
Remembered thy beauty for more than a day.
In the name of the truth from thy brow is torn
The crown of redemption thou long hast worn,
And into the valley of sin thou art hurled
To be trampled anew by the feet of the world.

The beautiful picture is thine no more
That hangs in the palace on Italy's shore;
The tear-stained eyes where the shadow lies,
Like a darksome cloud in the summer skies,
Will tell thy story to men no more,
For all untrue is the tale of yore;
And the far-famed picture that hangs on the wall
Is a painter's fancy—that is all.

Italia's shore is a land of light
Where the sunlight of day drowns the shadows of night;
And the great warm sun with his golden rays
Imprisons the light of eternal days;
But the tale of thy woes is a shadow there
That fills with its horror the perfumed air.

By day and by night in the palace there,
Thy picture has hung with its face so fair;

Beguiling the travelers come from afar
With its sad, sweet grace, like some voiceless star,
Till the hearts that shuddered before thy sin
Recalled not the shadow that lay within,
But remembered only with pitying grace
The hopeless grief on the child-like face.

The rosy dawn with its misty light,
Shone fair on thy brow in the morning bright;
And the glittering noon with its rays of gold
Imprisoned thy soul in its jewelled hold.

Oh, fair was the picture at early dawn,
With the matchless beauty that Guido had drawn;
And fair was the face in the noon of gold,
Touched with a glory that never grew old.

But lovelier still in the shadowed eyes
Lay the burning sunset of Italy's skies;
And the beautiful face with its voiceless woe
Grew fair as a saint's in the crimson glow.
No wonder the poets grew wild at the sight,
And sung of thy beauty with mad delight,
Till the fame of the picture spread over the land,
Revealing the touch of its master-hand.

The fair Madonna with saint-like face,
Creation of Raphael's exquisite grace,

Is scarcely more famed than the child-like head
Of thou to whom sorrow forever is wed.
O beautiful woman, the world with its scorn
Will mock at the glory thou long hast worn,
And rend aside in the name of the truth
The veil of mercy that hides thy youth.
But the romance that clings to the wondrous face
Will fall on our hearts with a softened grace,
And the fair young sinner on Italy's shore
Will be loved and pitied forevermore.

———

## UNDER THE STARS.

Under the stars, when the shadows fall,
    Under the stars of night;
What is so fair as the jewelled crown
Of the azure skies, when the sun is down,
    Beautiful stars of light!

Under the stars, where the daisies lie
    Lifeless beneath the snow;
Lovely and pure, they have lived a day,
Silently passing forever away,
    Lying so meek and low.

Under the stars in the long-ago—
    Under the stars to-night;

Life is the same, with its great unrest
Wearily throbbing within each breast,
    Searching for truth and light.

Under the stars as they drift along,
    Far in the azure seas;
Beautiful treasures of light and song,
Glad'ning the earth as they glide along,
    What is so fair as these?

Under the stars in the quiet night,
    Under the stars above;
Sweet is the breath of the evening air,
Spirits of heaven unseen are there,
    Weaving a web of love.

Under the stars in the shadowy eve,
    Glittering stars of truth; .
Beautiful sprays of eternal light,
Laid on the brow of the dusky night,
    Blossoms of fadeless youth.

———

## CATCHING THE SUNBEAMS.

Catching the sunbeams, oh, wee dimpled child,
    Gleefully laughing because they are bright;

Knowing, ah! never, my beautiful pet,
  Ne'er can our fingers imprison the light.


Beautiful sunshine, oh! fair is the light
  Falling on earth from the heavens above;
Beautiful childhood, oh! glad is the sight
  Filling the world with its measure of love.


Playing with sunbeams, oh, all of us, pet,
  Toy with the treasures, so shining and bright;
Catching the sunshine we never may hold,
  Trying, like you, to imprison the light.


Sunbeams that glitter and sparkle and shine—
  Life is so full of the beautiful light;
Gilding the wings of each fleet-footed day
  Only to fade in the shadows of night.


Playing with sunbeams, oh! all of us, pet,
  Long for the treasures so shining and glad;
Finding too late that they slip from our hands,
  Leaving us heart-sick and weary and sad.


Learning the lessons we never will heed—
  Life is so full of the things that we crave;
Catching the sunshine oh, darling, each heart
  Longs for the sunbeams till it reaches the grave.

## THE SOLDIER'S GRAVE.

[To the memory of Lieut. Wm. W. Wardell, of the First Massachusetts Cavalry, killed May 28, 1864.]

Above his head the cypress waves
    Its dark green drooping leaves ;
The sunlight through its branches wide
Where bright birds linger side by side
    A golden net-work weaves.

Within the church-yard's silent gloom
    He lies in quiet rest ;
And never more to cold, pale brow,
Or proud lips mute with silence now
    Will loving lips be pressed.

Perhaps even now in death's dark dream
    He sees the deadly strife ;
Where brothers fought with blinded eyes,
Forgetting all the tender ties
    That bound them life to life.

Ah ! nobly there he proudly rode
    With honest, warm, true heart ;
And shrank not from the carnage red,
But bravely there, among the dead,
    He took a soldier's part.

Yet soon his hands fell helplessly,
    Low at his trembling side ;
For on his brow the death drops rose,
While in his heart the life-blood froze
    And died his young life's pride.

The dark brown eyes, whose loving glance
    Gave happiness to all,
Have closed their weary lids for aye
Beneath the sunset of life's day,
    Where dark'ning shadows fall.

Oh, weary years that still creep on
    Adown the sands of Time,
Give back the loving tones of yore,
That haunt us here forever more,
    As echoing church bell's chime.

And yet it cannot, cannot be
    That hearts must ever grieve ;
Above his head the shadows fall,
Yet still the sunbeams shine through all
    And mystic splendors weave.

And thus upon the grieving heart
    That ever weeps for him,
The dark clouds fall, yet God's sweet light
Of faith still onward takes its flight,
    Through shadows vast and grim.

7

Oh! faint heart, with thy clinging grief,
    Look upward to the sky;
For there, beyond the weary strife,
Where angels ever guard thy life,
    There's One who hears thy cry.

Within the " City of the Dead "
    He only lies asleep ;
And soon his hand will clasp once more
Thine own as oft he did of yore,
    With love's pure feeling deep.

———

## BEYOND THE SUNSET ARE THE HILLS OF GOD.

Gleaming folds of red and gold linger in the western sky ;
Fleecy clouds of purest tint, mingle with the purple dye.

Faintly to the dreamy mind comes the sound of earthly life ;
Far beyond the shining banks, cometh rest from worldly
    strife.

Through the sunset's misty veil, now we look with longing
    eyes,
To behold more beauteous sight than the evening's glori-
    ous skies.

Slowly now the red banks part, showing what is hidden there ;
Flashing hills of shadowy light, piercing through the dark-
      'ning air.

Like the rainbow's promise clear, God has placed His em-
      blem there,
Giving life and trust to all, love unbounded, rich and rare.

Glimpses of a life beyond come to each faint, weary heart,
And we long for that bright shore where the loved ones
      ne'er shall part.

Strange, that souls should still live on, hopeless with their
      hidden pain ;
When, would they but read the skies, heaven and hope
      would come again.

Though the life be weary spent, evening brings the glory
      near ;
And beyond the sunset's glow, grand the hills of God appear.

---

## NEVER.

Two dark-brown eyes looked into mine
    Two eyes with restless quiver ;
A gentle hand crept in my own
    Beside the gleaming river.

" Ah, sweet," I murmured, passing sad,
　　You will forget me ever ? "
The dear, brown eyes their answer gave ;
　　" I will forget you *never*."

Up in the leaves above our heads
　　The winds were softly dying ;
Down in the river at our feet
　　The lilies pale were lying.
The winds their mournful murmur sent :
　　You will forget me ever ?
The lilies raised their drooping heads :
　　We will forget you never.

A spell hung o'er the numbered hours
　　That chained each thought and feeling ;
My heart was filled with idle dreams
　　That sent my senses reeling.
Once more I murmured. " Well. I know
　　You will forget me ever : "
Yet still the same dear promise came,
　　" I will forget you *never*."

Ah, vain the words that we must speak,
　　Though we are still believing ;
And subtle are the webs of fate
　　That love is ever weaving ;
The dark brown eyes meet mine no more,

I am forgotten ever;
And mocking memory echoes now,
   I will forget you *never.*

Beside the idle stream I stand,
   Where flowers droop and shiver·
And cold and dark it seems to me
   This dreary, restless river;
For, sweet, your eyes are lost to me,
   I am forgotten ever;
And only *memory* echoes now,
   " I will forget you *never.* "

----

## THE MISSISSIPPI.

Where is the bard, O river grand and old,
That has thy praises sung, thy beauties told,
In measures lofty as the mighty pride
That lingers in thy deep and flowing tide?
And where the echoing measures low and sweet
That should thine own faint rippling songs repeat?

The eyes of nature ever turned on thee
Watch o'er thy restless wandering to the sea;
The rosy morn awakes thee from thy sleep;
Along thy dusky waves her glances creep,

And o'er the weird dark shadows of the night
She spreads her sunny robes of morning light.

The yellow noon comes too, with fiery eyes,
And all unwept the dewy morning dies ;
Thy waters run in waves of rippling gold,
And all the rivers sacred deemed of old
Are not so grand as thee, nor yet so fair.
Amid the mists that fill the evening air
The sun droops low his golden head and dies,
Yet in thy depths his last glance ling'ring lies
And lights it with a royal purple glow ;
Anon into a splendor falling low
Of crimson stains and gleams of molten gold
It changes, like great waves of fire rolled
Across the sky.

       The moon caresses thee
With rays of silver light as to the sea
Thy dark waves glide ; and shadows long and wide
Reflect grim images within thy tide.
Pale stars that wander through the trackless skies
All night, glance in thy depths with glowing eyes,
And like a stream of silver flecked with gold
Thy waters run.
       O river, proud and old,
From snow-bound shores thy dark waves loosened run
To mingle with the waters of the sun ;

And lo! from North and South, from East and West,
Companions come to aid thee in thy quest.

Along thy shores great cities stately stand,
Sprung up beneath thy kindly welcoming hand;
Proud commerce lives upon thy sweeping tide
And palaces upon thy bosom glide.

O Mississippi, monarch of the West,
What daring hand can quell thy proud unrest ?
What human pen can paint thee as thou art,
The loved, the pride of every free-born heart ?
Thou symbol of a nation strong and free,
Whose throne is on the land and on the sea !
What power is thine, what might is unto thee !
Though men shall die, thy waters still will be.

---

## THE PRINCE IMPERIAL.

Under the cross in the Southern skies,
Where the beautiful night like a shadow lies,
A fair young life went out in the light
To wake no more in the star-crowned night.

Beautiful visions of life were his,
  Visions of triumph and fame ;

Longing for glory that he might be
    Worthy to wear his name.

Brave was his heart as he sailed away
    Under the Northern sky;
Leaving behind him all that he loved—
    Stilling his heart's wild cry.

Proudly his mother, with royal pride,
    Stifled her last regret;
Steeling her heart—but her dream was vain
    For the star of his race was set.

Surely the moon as he slept at night
    Whispered his doom on high;
Surely the waves in their rocky beds
    Mourned as he passed them by.

For never again in the dusky night
    Would the prince go sailing by;
Weaving his dreams with a boyish pride
    Under the shadowy sky.

Silent and cold in the morn he lay,
    Slain by a ruthless hand!
Never to wake with his fearless eyes—
    Never again to command.

Imperial mother—too well we know
    The speechless depths of her awful woe;

For the bright young life into Eternity hurled
Was her only link to a sad, dark world.

But mothers kneel in the silent night
To whisper a prayer to the Throne of Light,
For the beautiful woman whose head lies low,
Crushed 'neath the weight of its crown of woe.

From sun to shadow her life has swayed
Like some wild rose in a mountain glade :
But the storms have won, and the blossom lies
Forever broken—no more to rise.

--------

## ON THE LAKE.

There's a beautiful lake where the sun lies low,
And the skies are warm with their summer glow ;
And a beautiful picture there I see
Where the winds are warm and the waves are free,
    And the waves lie still in the sun
As the flowers at night, when the day is done.

You may sing of your silvery seas by night
When the moon looks down with a dreamy light ;
And the stars shine out in the skies above
Like the warm sweet gaze of the eyes of love ;

But the glow on the lake to-day
Is a glory that never will fade away.

The beautiful lake is a sea of gold
And the beauty it wears will never grow old;
The trees bend down in the sun's warm glow
Till their branches meet in the waves below,
     And the clouds in the far-off skies
Are mirrored anew where the sunlight lies.

I love to float where the shadows lie
'Neath the matchless glow of the summer sky;
And I love to dream that these waves of light
Will never fade in the gloomy night:
     But I know that the things I love
Are as far from my reach as the clouds above.

Oh, the beautiful lake is a sea of gold
And the beauty it wears will never grow old;
The cloudlets of Heaven are mirrored there
In a golden splendor so bright and fair
     That the soul is dazzled for aye
By the beautiful light of this summer's day.

Oh, I love to dream when this life is o'er
We shall moor our boats near the golden shore;
And our sorrows shall drift from us far away
As the leaves that float in their idle play,
     And the waves shall smile in the sun
When the night is over and life is done.

## BEYOND.

Beyond yon dim old mountain's shadowy height,
  The restless sun droops low his grand old face;
While downward sweeps the trembling veil of night,
  To hide the earth; the frost king's filmy lace
Rests on the mountain's hoary snow-crowned head,
  And adds to it a softened grace; the light
Which dies afar in faint and fading red
  In purple shadows circles near.

           The flight
Of birds across the vast and silent plains
  Awakes the echoes of the sleeping earth;
Of all the summer beauty naught remains,
  There come no tidings of the spring's glad birth.

Beyond the valley and the far-off height
  The birds in wandering do take their way;
Ah, whither is their strange and trackless flight
  Amid the dying embers of the day;
Into the clouds that seek to veil the sun
  They seem to float on strange bright wings of fire;
Beyond the shades that tell us day is done
  They soar on spirit wings that never tire.

Ah, strange, strange mysteries indeed are these;
  To watch the sunlight fade and die away,

To hear the whispering of the dark pine trees,
    To see the deepening shadows 'round us play,
And then to feel that all that 'round us lies
    Is e'en beyond the knowledge of the soul.
We seek to grasp the truth, it quickly flies
    And leaves us full of doubt.

                        Around us roll
The spheres that light the way to heaven's shore,
    And soon their lights will brighten all the sky;
And yet we dare not read their mystic lore
    But only stand and wait and wonder why,
Beyond, beyond in deep mysterious space
    They wander through the darkness all the night,
Each one within its own allotted place.

    The stars' dim course, the birds' lone dreamy flight,
Will ever fill our souls with doubt and fear.
    We walk upon life's unknown shadowy shore
With wandering steps, while through the heavens clear
    The stars their music sing forevermore.

---

## A SONNET.

Sweet summer queen, with trailing robe of green,
What spell hast thou to bind the heart to thee?

Thy throne is built upon the sun-lit sea,
Where break the waves in clouds of silver sheen
And oft at dawn like some resplendent queen,
Thou sittest on the hills in majesty ;
And all the flowers wake at thy decree.
But now farewell to all thy joys serene ;
The autumn comes with swift-winged, silent flight,
And he will woo thee with his fiery breath ;
In crimson robes and hues of flashing gold
He'll clothe thee, and thy beauty in the night
Will take a richer glow.   But wintry death
Will come and wrap thee in his fold.

---

## UNDER THE SEA.

Under the sea, the great wide sea
  That sweeps the golden shore ;
What treasures lie beneath the waves
      Forevermore !

Ask of the winds, the sobbing winds
  That toss the waves on high :
And fling the burden of their song
      Unto the sky.

Ask of the stars, the jewelled stars
  That sleep within the tide ;

Like golden lilies floating far,
         And swinging wide.

Ask of the clouds that drift at noon
  In fadeless seas of blue,
And looking down see skies beneath
         Of deeper hue.

Up in the sky, the golden clouds
  Will never make reply;
Deep in the sea, the jewelled stars
         In silence lie.

Under the sea, the great wide sea
  That sweeps the golden shore,
Are secrets hidden from us now
         And evermore.

————

## THE OLD YEAR AND THE NEW.

Low at my feet there lies to-night
  A crushed and withered rose;
Within its heart of fading red
  No crimson fire glows;
For o'er its leaves the frost of death
  Steals like an icy breath;

And soon 't will vanish from my sight,
   A thing of gloom and death.


Ah! beauteous flower, once thou wert
   My pleasure and my pride;
And now when thou art old and worn
   I will not turn aside;
But gently o'er thy faded leaves
   I'll shed one kindly tear;
That thou wilt know, though dead and gone,
   To memory thou art dear.


Before my gaze there lies to-night
   A rose-bud fresh and fair;
And like the breath of dewy morn
   Its fragrance scents the air.
This fragile flower I fain would pluck
   With hand most kind yet bold;
And watch its petals day by day
   Their shining wealth unfold.


And soon 'twill be my very own
   To keep forevermore:
This flower that bloomed for me alone
   Upon a heavenly shore.
God grant my hands may guard it well
   And keep it pure and fair;
For angel hands have gathered it
   And placed it in my care.

Then fare thee well, thou dying year,
    Thou art my withered rose;
And on the stem where once thou wert,
    Another flower grows;
Yet fear thee not, when thou art dead,
    To thee I'll still be true;
And 'mid the joys of other years
    I still will think of you.

---

## EASTER.

Let all the flowers wake to life;
    Let all the songsters sing;
Let everything that lives on earth
    Become a joyous thing.

Wake up, thou pansy, purple-eyed,
    And greet the dewy spring;
Swell out, ye buds. and o'er the earth
    Thy sweetest fragrance fling.

Why dost thou sleep, sweet violet?
    The earth has need of thee;
Wake up and catch the melody
    That sounds from sea to sea.

Ye stars, that dwell in noonday skies,
   Shine on, though all unseen;
The great White Throne lies just beyond,
   The stars are all between.

Ring out, ye bells, sweet Easter bells,
   And ring the glory in;
Ring out the sorrow, born of earth—
   Ring out the stains of sin.

O banners wide, that sweep the sky,
   Unfurl ye to the sun;
And gently wave above the graves
   Of those whose lives are done.

Let peace be in the hearts that mourn—
   Let " Rest " be in the grave;
The Hand that swept these lives away
   Hath power alone to save.

Ring out, ye bells, sweet Easter bells,
   And ring the glory in;
Ring out the sorrow, born of earth—
   Ring out the stains of sin.

## MAY.

The world is full of gems to-day,
   The world is full of love;
The earth is strewn with star-gemmed flowers
   That fall from skies above.

The sunshine is a stream of gold
   That flows from flower to flower;
The shadows are but passing thoughts
   That mark each shining hour.

The pansy nods her purple head,
   And sings a silent song;
Her life is full of sunny hours—
   The days are never long.

The rose uplifts her sun-crowned head;
   She is the queen of love;
Her eyes behold the hidden stars
   That glow in skies above.

There is a fragrance in the air,
   A glory in the sky;
Oh, who would sigh for other days,
   Or grieve for things gone by?

## SUMMER RAIN.

Oh, what is so pure as the glad summer rain,
That falls on the grass where the sunlight has lain?
And what is so fair as the flowers that lie
All bathed in the tears of the soft summer sky?

The blue of the heavens is dimmed by the rain
That wears away sorrow and washes out pain;
But we know that the flowers we cherish would die
Were it not for the tears of the cloud-laden sky.

The rose is the sweeter when kissed by the rain,
And hearts are the dearer where sorrow has lain;
The sky is the fairer that rain-clouds have swept,
And no eyes are so bright as the eyes that have wept.

Oh, they are so happy, these flowers that die,
They laugh in the sunshine, oh, why cannot I?
They droop in the shadow, they smile in the sun,
Yet they die in the winter when summer is done.

The lily is lovely, and fragrant her breath,
But the beauty she wears is the emblem of death;
The rain is so fair as it falls on the flowers,
But the clouds are the shadows of sunnier hours.

Why laugh in the sunshine, why smile in the rain?
The world is a shadow and life is a pain;

Why live in the summer, why dream in the sun,
To die in the winter, when summer is done ?

Oh, there is the truth that each life underlies,
That baffles the poets and sages so wise;
Ah ! there is the bitter that lies in the sweet
As we gather the roses that bloom at our feet.

Oh, flowers forgive me, I'm willful to-day,
Oh, take back the lesson you gave me I pray;
For I slept in the sunshine, I woke in the rain
And it banished forever my sorrow and pain.

## SEPTEMBER.

Oh, soon the forests all will boast
    A crown of red and gold ;
A purple haze will circle round
    The mountains dim and old ;
Afar the hills, now green and fair,
    Their sombre robes will wear;
A mist-like veil will dim the sun
    And linger on the air.

Already seems the earth half sad
    The summer-child is dead;
And who can tell the dreams gone by,
    The tales of life unsaid?

September is a glowing time ;
  A month of happy hours :
Yet in its crimson heart lies hid
  The frost that kills the flowers.


Life, too, may feel the glory near
  And wear its crown of gold ;
Yet are the snows not nearest then ?
  Are hearts not growing old ?
September is the prime of life,
  The glory of the year :
Yet when the leaves begin to fall
  The winter must be near.

———    •

## OCTOBER.

I would not ask thee back, fair May,
  With all your bright-eyed flowers ;
Nor would I welcome April days
  With all their laughing showers ;
For each bright season of the year
  Can claim its own sweet pleasures ;
And we must take them as they come—
  These gladly-given treasures.

There's music in the rain that falls
   In bright October weather;
And we must learn to love them both—
   The sun and rain together.
A mist is 'round the mountain-tops
   Of gold-encircled splendor;
A dreamy spell is·in the air
   Of beauty sad and tender.


The winter hath not wooed her yet,
   This fair October maiden;
And she is free to wander still
   With fruits and flowers laden.
She shakes the dew-drops from her hair
   In one swift, golden shower;
And all the woods are filled with light
   That gilds each autumn flower.


But soon the frost-king's icy breath
   Will chill her laughing beauty;
And she will waken in the dusk
   Unto a sterner duty.
Ah! life is full of days like these,
   Of days too bright to perish;
Yet death, like winter, claims too oft
   The things we most would cherish.

## FALLING LEAVES.

There was a sound of music low—
　An undertone of laughter ;
The song was done, and can't you guess
　The words that followed after ?

Like autumn leaves sometimes they fall—
　The words that burn and falter ;
And is it true they too must fade
　Upon Love's sacred altar ?

From memory each one of us
　Can cull some sweetest treasure ;
Yet golden days, like golden leaves,
　Give pain as well as pleasure.

There was a sound of music low—
　An undertone of laughter :
The sun was gone—yet heaven knew
　The stars that followed after.

---

## AUTUMN FLOWERS.

O crimson-tinted flowers
　That live when others die,

What thoughtless hand unloving
　　Could ever pass you by?

You are the last bright blossoms,
　　The summer's after-glow,
When all her early children
　　Have faded long ago.

Sweet golden-rod and xenia
　　And crimson marigold,
What dreams of autumn splendor
　　Your velvet leaves unfold.

Long, long ago the violets
　　Have closed their sweet blue eyes,
And lain with pale, dead faces
　　Beneath the summer skies.

And on their graves you blossom
　　With leaves of gold and red,
And yet—how soon forever
　　Your beauty will be fled.

The frost will come to kill you,
　　The snows will wrap you round;
And you will sleep forgotten
　　Upon the frozen ground.

Your tints are like the beauty
    The sunlight leaves behind,
And deep and full of sadness
    The thoughts you bring to mind.

Dear memories of the summer!
    Sweet tokens of the past!
You are the fairest flowers
    Because you are the last.

---

## REMEMBRANCE.

Why should we dream of days gone by?
    Why should we wait and wonder?
Sweet summer days have come and gone,
    The leaves are falling yonder.

The wee sweet flowers we loved the best,
    The king of frost has chosen;
And now the sun looks sadly down
    Upon his darlings frozen.

Ah! summer sun and autumn frost.
    You are at war forever;
For all the ties that one would make
    The other fain would sever.

With autumn days remembrance comes
　　Of golden glories fleeting;
Of pleasures gone and sorrows come—
　　Of parting and of meeting.

Oh! summer days, why haunt us still?
　　Remembrance is a sorrow;
And all the dreams we dream to-day
　　Will fade upon the morrow.

Each life has some sweet summer-time,
　　Some perfect day of beauty;
When flowers of love and leaves of hope
　　Are twined around each duty.

But oh! the autumn-time will come,
　　When fades each golden glory;
And life, when we are old and gray,
　　Seems but a sad, old story.

————

## WINTER FLOWERS.

The summer queen has many flowers
　　To deck her sunny hair,
And trailing grasses, pure and sweet,
　　To scent the heavy air;
And upward through the misty sky

There is a glory, too,
Of floating clouds and rifts of gold
And depths of smiling blue.

Yet winter, too, can boast a wealth
Of flowers pure and white;
A kingly crown of frosted gems—
A wreath of sparkling light;
So bright and beautiful, indeed,
It were a wondrous sight
To see a world of fragile flowers
Sprung up within a night.

And sometimes there are cast'es, too,
Of glittering ice and snow,
Piled high upon our window-panes
'Neath curtains hanging low;
And they are like the castles fair
Our day-dreams build for aye;
A frozen mist that one warm breath
May quickly drive away.

And yet, how beautiful they are,
These flowers of our breath :
That bloom when not a leaf is left
To mourn the summer's death.
And oh ! how wondrous are the things
That God has given the earth;

The day that brings to one a death
Smiles on another's birth.

---

## SNOW-FLAKES

I wonder what they are,
   These pretty, wayward things,
That o'er the gloomy earth
   The wind of heaven flings.

Each one a tiny star,
   And each a perfect gem;
What magic in the art
   That thus has fashioned them.

What beauty in the flake
   That falls upon my hand;
And yet this tiny thing
   My will cannot command.

No two are just alike,
   And yet they are the same;
I wonder if my thought
   Could give to each a name.

Unlike the fragile flowers
   That love the sun's warm rays,

These snow-flakes love the cold,
  And die on sunny days!

So dainty and so pure,
  How beautiful they are;
And yet the slightest touch
  Their purity may mar.

They must be gazed upon,
  Not handled or caressed;
And thus we hold afar
  The things we love the best.

---

## SUNSET ON THE MISSISSIPPI.

O beautiful hills in the purple light,
  That shadow the western sky,
I dream of you oft in the silent night,
  As the golden days go by.

The river that flows at my longing feet
  Is tinged with a deeper glow;
But the song that it sings is as sad to-day
  As it was in the long ago.

The far-off clouds in the far-off sky
  Are tinted with gold and red;

But the lesson they tell to the hearts of men
  Is a lesson that never is said.


The star-crowned night in her sable plumes
  Is veiling the eastern sky,
And she trails her robes in the dying fires
  That far in the west do lie.


A single gem from her circlet old
  Is lost as she wanders by,
And the beautiful star with its golden light
  Shines out in the lonely sky.


O beautiful star in the misty sky,
  My soul would take wings with thee;
But you sail away in your golden seas
  With never a thought for me.


O sun-crowned hills in the purple light.
  I could sit at your feet forever;
But you fade away in the shadowy night
  And I'll see you again, ah, never.


Dark river that flows at my longing feet,
  I list to your music low;
But the song that you sing brings me thoughts to-night
  Of the beautiful long ago;

And my soul grows sad as I think of the day—
    That radiant day of light—
When the sun went down in a glory of gold
    'Neath the pitiless shadows of night.

Farewell, ye hills in the purple light;
    Farewell to your glory forever;
You fade away in the silent night,
    And I'll see you again, ah, never!

## NOT DEAD, BUT SLEEPING.

[To the memory of Edwin B. Foster, a member of the Howards, who nobly sacrified his own life for others, and in remembrance of those unknown to fame or friends who have silently followed in the steps of our Saviour.]

The shadow of death is around us all,
    And life is a sorrowful thing;
For the winds sweep by with a mournful sigh,
    And sad are the tidings they bring.

He is dead—and the strong, brave life that he gave
    Seemed offered to God in vain;
Yet he died, Christ-like, in a labor of love,
    'Mid sorrow and death and pain.

And why should we sorrow—the crown is his
 And the glory of life is won ;
Though he died when his labor was just begun,
 Yet the work of his life is done.

The beautiful South is a land of death,
 Where the shadows darken the sun ;
And the moans of the dying are heard in the night
 When the deeds of the day are done.

The sunlight falls with a dreary gleam
 On the cities where ruin is spread,
And the rain beats down with a mournful sound
 On the graves of the silent dead.

Yet high in the heavens a Hand is stretched,
 That treasures the deeds of love ;
And the lives gone out in the darkness below
 Are wrapped in the glory above.

The North bends down in her icy pride
 And kisses the land of the sun ;
Love joins them both in a flood of tears,
 And the glory of peace is won.

The hand that was dyed in a brother's blood
 Now eases that brother's pain ;
And the hearts that in life were driven apart,
 In death are united again.

Then why should we sorrow—our God is love,
   And lives are not lived in vain ;
Bright hope still shines like a star of night
   In the shadow of death and pain.

---

## A SUNBEAM.

The sun was hid all day by clouds,
   The rain fell softly down ;
A cold gray mist hung o'er the earth,
   And veiled the silent town.

Behind the clouds a sunbeam crept
   With restless wings of gold ;
The skies above were bright and warm,
   The earth below was cold.

It glanced along the heavy clouds,
   Then sought to glide between ;
But ah ! they gathered closer still,
   With fierce and angry mien.

The dancing ray grew strangely still,
   Just like some weary bird,
That droops upon a lonely shore,
   And sings its song unheard.

9

For on the earth the drooping flowers
    Were longing for the light;
And children with their watching eyes
    Could trace no sunbeam's flight.

At last an angel, wand'ring by,
    With snowy wings outspread,
Beheld the sunbeam sad at heart,
    And passing by she said:

" Why wait you here above the clouds,
    The earth has need of you;
Spread out your wings, speed quickly on
    And pierce the vapor through."

But still the sunbeam mournfully
    Gazed on the gloom below;
Then looked up in the spirit's face
    With softened, anxious glow.

The angel smiled, the clouds gave way
    And drifted far apart;
And lo! the glory of that smile
    Fell on each earthly heart.

Then quickly through the widening rift
    The sunbeam drifted down:
A ray of gold fell through the mist
    Upon the silent town.

Two weary eyes beheld its light,
  Then closed forevermore;
A soul passed through the rift of blue
  And reached the farther shore.


One moment o'er the wan, white face
  A ray of glory fell;
Then shadows came, the sunbeam fled;
  Its future who can tell?


Once more the clouds enwrapped the earth,
  The rain fell softly down;
A cold, gray mist hung o'er the hills
  And veiled the silent town.

# THE PHANTOM OF LOVE.

SHE stood by my side with a queenly air,
Her face it was young and proud and fair;
She held my rose in her hands of snow:
It crimsoned her face with a deeper glow;
The sunlight drooped in her eyes of fire
And quickened my heart to a wild desire;
I envied the rose in her hands so fair,
I envied the flowers that gleamed in her hair.

Ah! many a suitor I knew before
Had knelt at her feet in the days of yore;
And many a lover as foolish as I,
Had proudly boasted to win or die.
She had scorned them all with a careless grace
And a woman's scorn on her beautiful face.
Yet now in the summer I knelt at her feet,
And dreamed a dream that was fair and sweet.

The roses drooped in her gold-brown hair,
And quivered and glowed in the sun-lit air;
The jewels gleamed on her hands of snow
And dazzled my eyes with their fitful glow.
A river of gold ran low at our feet,

And echoed the words I cannot repeat.
Oh! life was so fair that I loved the sun!
And love was so sweet when the day was done!

The sun in her velvety eyes looked down
And deepened their glow to a warmer brown.
I loved this woman, this woman so fair,
With her sun-lit eyes and her gleaming hair;
I drank in her beauty as men drink wine,—
It filled my soul with a love divine.
The touch of her hand was madness to me;
Oh, my love was as great as love could be!

I kissed the roses that drooped in her hair,
I pressed the dews from her lips so fair;
I held her hands in my own once more;
Oh, never was woman so loved before!
And what did we care that the sun was low,
And the hills were bright with the sunset glow?
The purple that glowed in the skies above,
Was the royal banner of hope and love.

One perfumed breath from her lips so fair,
One sacred kiss on her sun-lit hair,
And then we parted as lovers meet—
I gathered the roses that lay at her feet,
And fastened them in, with a lover's prayer,
Where she loved them best, in her silken hair;

For the things she loved were as dear to me
As the shining stars to the watching sea.

On lake and river, the sun lay low
Where we parted that night in the summer glow
And the hanging clouds were steeped in red,
That rivalled the gold of her sun-crowned head.
And I loved her best as I saw her last.
With the beautiful colors floating past,
And the soft warm light in her velvety eyes,
Reflecting the glow of the sun-kissed skies.

*       *       *       *       *       *

I stood on the shore when the moon hung low
And shone on the clouds like the sun on snow;
And a midnight silence filled the air
As I gazed on the river, calm and fair.
I stood alone where the dark reeds quiver,
And the lilies pale in the night-winds shiver.
I dreamed of my love that was fair as the day,
Oh, the beautiful love that would last for aye!

Oh! what is that—in the river there—
Is it the gleam of the lilies tall and fair,
Or only the branch of some fallen tree,
By the constant wash of the waves set free?
Oh, see! how strange it looks and how white.
How it glistens and gleams in the shining light!
It dazzles my eyes—Oh, what can it be?
It is nearing the shore—it is coming to me!

My God! that my eyes could be blind to-night
To shut out forever that dreadful sight!
Oh. God! am I mad—or can it be
That the woman I loved is thus coming to me?
That bright thing drifting down with the tide,
Is all that is left of my beautiful bride!

Oh, pitiless moon with your pale cold light,
Grow dark for one instant and shut out that sight,
Till my eyes, grown dim with their tears unshed
Shall look no more on the face of my dead.

The pale lilies circle around her head
And whisper slowly—my love is dead.
The dark weeds lie in her tangled hair,
Where I last saw the roses gleaming there.
The cold winds shiver and moan in the night
As they sweep 'round her brow in the shining light.
Oh. God! is it I who am standing alone
Where the night-winds shiver and creep and moan,
Filling my soul with a grief so mad
That I hate the things that are living and glad?

Fear not. my love, you shall welcome be,
For even in death you have come to me.
The dead and the living shall lie to-night
'Neath the pitiless waves of that river bright.

I grasp her robe as it sweeps me by—
We have lived together, together we die;
Her face is so white—is it a woman I see,
Or only a phantom drifting past me?
Her hand is so near—it touches my own—
My God! it is gone—I am standing alone.

Oh, why did I love when the sun was high,
And the clouds lay piled in the glittering sky!
Oh, why did I love when the sun lay low
And the heavens were red with the blood-red glow!
And why do I live when the purple light
Is faded forever from out of my sight.

Oh, beautiful demon, that men call love,
As fair as the angels that smile above!
'T were better that men should never be born
Than see thy face in the dewy morn.
'T were better that women should stand afar,
And worship in vain some cold, proud star;
Than drink in thy beauty with passionate breath
That brings to them only sorrow and death.